DIARY OF
A PROSECUTOR
ON THE RUN

DIARY OF A PROSECUTOR ON THE RUN

Stories

TYLER SCHIFF

Bottle Productions, LLC
Santa Monica, California

Author photo: © Beowulf Sheehan
Cover design: Richard Ljoenes

Contact:
Tylerschiffauthor@gmail.com
ISBN: 979-8-35094-149-4

To Mom, who filled my room with books.

This is a work of fiction.

Dear friends at the New York City Police Department,

On August 1, my long shift will be over. The first forty years I was in service to the city seemed to go by in a minute. The last two years were a blurry eternity. That's not a complaint; it's just the way the photograph of my life developed. I don't blame the era. I don't blame the body politic. I don't blame any god who failed to protect the interests of hardworking citizens. At this point, I don't blame. I just accept. I'm grateful for the time I spent and the friends I made here. I worked among common heroes. I saw the best of what you have to offer. As the great Tony Soprano said, "It's good to be in something from the ground floor. . . . But lately I'm getting the feeling that I came in at the end. That the best is over."

It might be true that the best is over. But I have the stories.

Many of you know about my Tuesday night story group. Seven p.m. on Tuesdays, I have the back two tables at Reservoir Tavern. I invite anyone I meet to join me on Tuesdays. To tell a story. Or just listen. There are no rules. The first beer is on me.

Which brings me here. If you're part of the New York City law enforcement family and we've worked together in any capacity, if you live nearby or play softball in the same league—if you're a friend of a friend—please consider submitting a tale, a memory, a story from your life and career. It can be anything. It can be your highest achievement or worst failure. It can be the moment after which everything changed in your life. It can be a time when you were bored beyond belief. It can be a day you felt pain, shame, fear, hunger, or humiliation. It can be joy.

Send your submission to the e-mail address here: Nlrice22@columbia.edu. Before my retirement party on August 21, I will collect the pieces you submit. I will add them to a black, three-ring binder. The stories will be on offer for anyone to read and enjoy. Afterward, I will keep them at my house. Please visit.

Lastly, if you want to contribute but don't feel your writing is good, my son-in-law is an English teacher. He will edit for free. If you'd prefer your submission to be anonymous, specify that in the e-mail.

As my daughter says, love and gratitude,
Arthur Macy

Records Dept. Supervisor, NYPD

Note from the Editor:

My father-in-law asked me to edit these pages. I have used a light touch.

If as you read this collection you find warts and blemishes—if the story doesn't hook and hold your interest, if tropes abound, if dialogue is false, pretentious or lacks purpose, if characters' private and hidden selves aren't revealed through choice and dilemma, if central plots and subplots don't weave together, if the second act drags or the climax disappoints or the resolution doesn't bring serenity to chaos,[1] if taste and judgment are flat, gone, lacking, nil, dead—if as you read through this collection of stories you find you are not enjoying them, then please remember this: These people have day jobs. They are patrolling your streets. They are cops. Attorneys. 9-1-1 operators. Crime-scene analysts. U.S. marshals. Court officers. Prison guards. Judges. They do not aspire to be writers. Their contribution was a gift to Arthur Macy, and so let it be just that: a gift. Let this stand as a memorial to my father-in-law's enjoyment of anyone who shares a good story without hubris.

Warmly,

Nelson Rice, PhD
Associate Professor of English
Nlrice22@columbia.edu

---

1 Special thanks to R. McKee for this list of story vulgaris.

Chapter One. Caitlin Rex

Mrs. Caitlin Rex rented a pleasant apartment, two rooms and kitchenette, in a canary yellow apartment building near the ocean in Santa Monica. On her last birthday when she turned sixty-one, she thought that no one her age should take a job assignment clear across the country in an unfamiliar zip code. But then why not? She was still excellent at her profession, her hand was steady, her eye for detail was perfect, her interview techniques were uncanny, and her use of color, shadow and nuance had brought hundreds of fugitives and unidentified criminals to the doorstep of justice. Plus, a change of scenery was welcome. She'd lived on the Upper West Side of New York City her entire life. Now she'd try California for a few weeks, and if it worked . . . well, she was getting ahead of herself.

She rose from bed and peered out the window at the butter yellow stucco walls. The building was built in the 1930s, when construction still mattered. The walls were thick, sturdy, and each window had an intricate scrimshaw pattern around the edge. She padded to the bathroom, where for the first time ever, she had a window seat. There was a tiny, jewel-box seat that looked out at a jacaranda tree. For the past two mornings, she'd sat on the cushion and combed her silver-white hair into a bob, clipped it back with a tortoiseshell clip, dabbed petroleum on the pads of her eyes, checked her nails and teeth for decay, and then, when she felt fresh, she got dressed to go down to the police station. Grey sweater set with pearl-colored buttons. Grey slacks. Grey windbreaker. Gold stud earrings. She left the gold cross necklace her husband gave her for their twenty-fifth wedding anniversary in its velvet pouch, because she didn't yet trust the streets of Santa Monica.

There was a Starbucks four blocks away, but she preferred to make coffee and toast in her rental. At the door, before she left, she slipped her FBI Identification Catalog, a tattered and battered copy, into her black leather briefcase. Then she locked the door behind her, went to her outdoor staircase and passed the jacaranda tree on her way out the gate. As she greeted the bus driver, took her seat behind him, and pressed her face to the window, as she rode the Big Blue Bus to work, she had the same thought three mornings in a row: *Why has it never occurred to me to live in California?* Maybe it was her immigrant parents. One was Persian, the other was French, and they were such serious people. They'd worked so *incredibly* hard to establish a life in New York City. It would never have occurred to them to leave New York for such a far-fetched place as California. Yes, that must be it, Caitlin thought as she passed the spiky palm trees, clean cement, runners, bikers, baby strollers, and shiny electric cars of Los Angeles. If she felt a tinge of regret, it reversed itself when she stepped off the bus.

The Santa Monica police station was an odd place. She'd spent her life in police stations—she thought she'd seen the lot—but here the booking officer looked stoned. Homeless people who were not under investigation, had not been arrested, drifted about. The electric doors opened for ghosts. The ocean breeze, which initially she'd enjoyed, carried the scent of trash and blood right into the lobby. As she entered and went to the employee bathroom to check her hair, she found a woman squatting in the hallway, pissing blue urine onto the tiles. No officer bothered to move her. Again, Caitlin thought the Santa Monica police station was a strange and foreign labyrinth. It was not a place where she could work on a permanent basis.

"How are you coming along?" Irwin Sanchez asked her when she entered his office that morning. Irwin was a burly man with most of his weight below his hips. He had a booming, voice, a haphazard smile, and a passive-aggressive swagger. Irwin paced in front of his big glass window with a crisscross of freeways framing his back. He unfurled the forensic map for Caitlin to see. The map was labeled "908 CHATWORTH LANE—CRIME SCENE 9.0—MURDER." The document was so large, so substantial that one corner dragged on the floor. It contained a high-watt color key, dimension lines and evidence markers.

"I'll start today. I'll meet the witness this morning," Caitlin said.

"How long will it take you to produce a sketch?" Irwin asked.

"A first draft or a final draft? Well. I guess it depends how the interview goes. If she's cooperative, if she listens and answers the questions, it should take me a few days."

"And if she's not cooperative?" Irwin asked, flexing up one eyebrow.

"Is she *not* cooperative?" Caitlin inquired.

"I dunno," Irwin said, turning to face the window.

"Irwin. It helps if you give me full information," Caitlin added.

"Here's some information. I'm in charge of the budget for this department. The budget is my number one priority. I submit our expenses to someone at City Hall on Friday every week, and on Monday, I get an angry person yelling at me on the phone. So as much as I respect your record, your thirteen hundred and twenty-two correct identifications, as much as I'd like to tell you that you have all the time in the world to complete this project, you don't. Because I have budget constraints. If you fail to submit a sketch by Wednesday, if you don't identify the person who murdered that girl's mother in three days, I'm afraid I'll need to put you on a plane," Irwin said.

"Wednesday? My rental goes through Friday," Caitlin piped.

"Wednesday is my Friday," Irwin said sternly.

Now Caitlin felt offput, as Irwin flashed his odd, lopsided smile at her. His upper lip didn't match his lower lip. He'd just thrown down the hammer and yet there he was, pretending to be a friendly, agreeable boss. Caitlin wondered if this was California behavior.

"What's wrong?" Irwin asked, sensing her angst.

"Nothing," Caitlin answered.

"Why don't I take you to the famous Mel's Diner for breakfast? It's right across the freeway. They have jukeboxes. Great short waffles. Good people-watching. Then we'll head over to 908 Chatworth Lane. You can meet the little girl."

"I've eaten," Caitlin said, reaching for her bag.

-

It was true, Caitlin Rex was one of the *best* forensic artists. She had lifetime-to-date 1,322 correct identifications. She'd been celebrated, interviewed, studied, copied, lauded, written up, even invited to the White House for cake in the Rose Garden after the faceless bomber was caught. She'd been called the forensic artist of her generation, and thus there was nothing she didn't know about forensic art. She'd interviewed blind and deaf witnesses. She'd taught courses at Quantico about interviewing witnesses who were withholding information. She'd sat with people so overwhelmed with grief that they couldn't form words, their memory was frozen, and she'd developed techniques that were used the world over to get grief-stricken mothers, daughters, grandmothers, neighbors, friends, lovers, bosses, and enemies to talk, loosen up, unlock the gates of memory. Caitlin wrote a book on nonverbal cues. She knew how to be patient. She knew when to be impatient. She could prod, coax, lure images from the mind onto the tongue. When she scribbled all this in her black Rollbahn notebook, when she went home to her table spread with pickle jars full of paintbrushes, when she sat at her easel and put pen, pencil, pastel to paper, no artist made a better rendering. Her lines, her details, were immaculate. They'd said this was so in a profile in *People* magazine, and she believed it.

Her only failing, if she had a failing, was that she didn't like children. She said it was for professional reasons that she never bore children; could a great forensic artist starve the world of her skill just to change diapers and rinse dishes and do laundry? No, certainly not, she told her husband in the quiet confines of their apartment with a view of the park one misty night in the 1970s. They'd never *really* considered children because the truth was that neither of them liked children. Or dogs. This was so deeply unpopular a view that they rarely spoke it aloud. Caitlin and her husband agreed to join in this secret, unpopular view, and all was well; it never impacted Caitlin's life or work, except when it did.

Today was one of those occasions.

-

"What's the name of this neighborhood?" Caitlin asked the bus driver.

"The obnoxious one," the bus driver said, jerking the gear. "Brentwood Park. It's a nice-sounding name but the people aren't anything like that. Repulsive people with repulsive children. Watch out for yourself—" he warned her as the bus hissed to a stop.

As she deboarded, Caitlin wondered about that bus driver and his inflexible ideas. She clasped her black leather bag under her elbow and made her way along the sidewalk in Brentwood Park. The box hedges thickened. The houses grew large. The driveways looped and turned with expensive little pebble gardens. Fountains trickled. Little dogs poked their manicured heads through gates. Caitlin thought it looked like a wonderful street in a sunny, leafy subsection of Los Angeles. Even as she neared 908 Chatworth Lane, covered in a tangle of yellow crime scene tape and bougainvillea—even as she counted the squad cars and forensics vans and news trucks blocking the driveway and expansive lawn—even as she took this in, she thought Brentwood Park looked like an idyllic place to grow up.

"How do you do, ma'am?" a cop called over.

"Where do I find the witness?" Caitlin called back.

"The eyewitness is in the backyard. Near the trampoline," the cop answered.

Caitlin combed the first floor of the house, taking note of every small detail and matching it to the map she'd photographed with her phone in Irwin Sanchez's office. She took an extra minute or two in the kitchen, where the crime scene investigators in yellow hazmat coveralls were sprawled on their bellies, inspecting every inch of the Spanish tile floor. One had a box of Q-tips and a magnifying glass. He was inspecting a bloodstain. Another had a pair of tongs and was apparently picking up microscopic fibers and bits of dirt.

"What are the dimensions of the bloodstain?" Caitlin asked one of them.

"The stain is exactly the length of the victim's body. Plus an inch. It starts here and extends past the oven into the pantry. Someone tried to wash part of it off with hand soap or dish soap, but then the person stopped. They abandoned the effort. We don't know why."

"Interesting—" Caitlin said, peering through the window over the sink. The view was into the leafy, green backyard. There was a middle-aged woman in a dark suit, her hair in tight curls, seated at the end of a chaise lounge. She talked to a girl, maybe seven or eight or nine years old—it was hard to tell because the woman in the suit blocked the view.

"Who is the eyewitness being interviewed by?" Caitlin asked.

"She's with Dr. Polly right now."

"Is Dr. Polly with the Santa Monica police?"

"No," the CSI said, lifting his head from the bloodstain. "Dr. Polly is a child psychiatrist. She's been with the family for a while. She's been here since yesterday at 8 a.m. She'll be glad for you to take over."

Caitlin touched a pink flag, an evidence marker, planted next to the weapon. The weapon, they suspected, was this black, twelve-pound Vitamix blender which was lying on its side on the kitchen floor. On one corner of the Vitamix blender, bits of hair and blood and yellow gunk were stuck. Caitlin had read all this in the report but didn't properly believe it until she saw it with her own eyes. *A Vitamix blender?* She wasn't supposed to take photos with her phone—there were strict rules and procedures about who could document the crime scene and where the files were stored, certainly not on personal devices—but she did it anyway. She snapped a photo quickly.

"What are you doing?" a little voice piped behind her.

Caitlin jumped an inch. Behind her, a tall and gangly seven- or eight- or nine-year-old appeared, with flouncy white curls hanging into her big, tear-stained, blue eyes. The girl was in a filthy Liberty print dress, and she held to her chest a package of sticky, gooey, yellow marshmallow ducks. As she stuffed a marshmallow duck into her mouth, a smile played on her lips. The girl knew she'd caught Caitlin breaking a rule.

"I'm Caitlin Rex. I'm a forensic artist. I came all the way from New York."

"That's not interesting," the girl chimed back.

Caitlin eyed the package of candy the girl clasped. "Are those from Easter?"

"Yes, my mother hid them and now I've just found them," the girl said gleefully. "Do you want to come play in the backyard with Dr. Polly?"

As the eyewitness skipped out the French doors that led to the patio and pool area, Caitlin followed closely behind. Dr. Polly was packing her things. She wore a funereal look on her face. Streaked red hair. Her eyebrows plucked out of existence.

"I quit. I'm done," Dr. Polly whispered, passing Caitlin brusquely.

"Are you leaving?" Caitlin asked. "Can I view your notes?"

There was no answer from Dr. Polly as she disappeared inside the house.

"She's no fun anyway!" the girl shouted back. She was now bouncing furiously on the trampoline. The candy was still in her grasp, even as she flipped over and back and over and back, her filthy dress billowing over her head to reveal long, skinny, dirt-stained legs.

"Can you tell me your name?" Caitlin called out to her.

"Are you another psychiatrist?" the girl asked.

"No, I promise you I'm not. I told you, I'm a forensic artist and I came here with a specific job to do. Now if you get down from the trampoline and sit with me, I promise I'll make it worth your while."

The girl understood a bribe as well as anything. She climbed down from the trampoline and stood across from Caitlin, where she littered the empty cellophane package on the ground. She ate the dregs, the yellow marshmallow goo, from under her nails.

"Cecily," the girl said.

"Cess-suh-lee," Caitlin repeated slowly. "Did I say it correctly?"

"Cess-suh-*lee*," the girl sung, putting stress on the last syllable.

Caitlin studied the girl more closely and noted she was sickly-looking. Her high forehead was beaded with sweat. She had spider veins running through her cheeks. Her vacant turquoise eyes had flecks of red. Her bleach-white curls hadn't been washed or combed. All over the front of her expensive Liberty print dress were smudges of dirt, grass, grape jelly, and now threads of yellow marshmallow goo. When the girl smiled, she revealed tiny, mustard-colored teeth, sharp as daggers, sticking down from inflamed gums. From a foot away, Caitlin could smell her sickly sweet foul breath.

"Thank you for telling me your name, Cecily," Caitlin said. "I've worked with many children before. Typically, I come to your home after a difficult event. I ask you questions about a terrible moment you witnessed, a traumatic event, and I ask you to describe things that you remember. I ask you to describe a person or persons you saw in that moment. From your words and memories and descriptions, I make a drawing."

"What kind of drawing?" Cecily asked.

"A portrait. It's a drawing of the suspect. We give that rendering to the police and it helps them catch the man who hurt your mother. Does that make sense to you?"

"Can I see what's in your bag?" Cecily had the gold latch open and was digging her sticky, filthy fingers through the bag.

"It's okay. You can look through my things," Caitlin said, feigning control over Cecily, who was unpacking, scattering her cherished items across the table. Two lined notebooks. Heavy sketchbook. Colored pens and pencils and pastels. Specialty erasers. Paintbrushes. Pickle jar for paintbrushes. Pickle jar for water. Battered copy of the FBI Identification Catalog. When Cecily found the FBI Identification Catalog, she stopped and became entranced. Mesmerized. She thumbed through the pages, admiring photographic descriptions of suspects with "egg-shaped" heads, "mouth grill" dental work, "braided beard," "disappearing" lips, "cleft" chin, "bugged-out" eyes. She giggled and pointed.

"Did you make all these drawings?" Cecily asked.

"No those are photographs of real people. Sometimes, if a witness can't describe a facial feature, I show them examples of that facial feature on a real person. Then they say *yes* or *no* and *yes* or *no*, and eventually, we make a whole face together."

"Let's do this! Let's do this!" Cecily shouted, losing volume control. She was so worked up that a trickle of pee came down her bare leg.

"Okay, try to settle down. It's not good to be in an excited state when we start to make this drawing. Cecily, can you take a seat? I'll get my list of questions. As I understand from my notes, last Monday at 9:30 p.m., a person or persons invaded your kitchen and bludgeoned your mother. Do you remember anything about this moment? Can you tell me what you noticed about the person? Did he or she remind you of someone your mother would be friends with? When the paramedics arrived, they found you standing in the kitchen. They had the idea that you saw everything that happened. Is that true?"

Cecily's eyes turned gloomy. "I'm bored—" she moaned.

"You're bored?" Caitlin asked.

"Yes, I'm bored. I want my iPad. I want my iPad!" Cecily shouted in crescendo.

Caitlin didn't expect for her patience to be tested this early in the process. She rose from her chair, took a deep breath, and stood a few inches taller than the girl. "Cecily, I flew all the way across the country to make a drawing of the suspect with you. If you sit and focus for just a few minutes, I'll do my best to get you through this process. Quickly. Painlessly. If you answer my list of questions, if you pick out facial features from that book you really like then we'll be finished by lunchtime. Is that a deal?"

A smile formed on Cecily's lips. Something had occurred to her, and now her focus was laser-sharp. She inched right next to Caitlin and motioned for her to bend down. When Caitlin did as she was asked, Cecily whispered hot breath in her ear. "I want you to come into the kitchen with me."

"It's a working crime scene. It's no place for a child," Caitlin said.

"I know, but I have something to show you," Cecily said.

-

Caitlin found Irwin Sanchez exactly where he'd started the workday, in his office at the big glass window that overlooked Interstate 10.

"Irwin, I have a problem," Caitlin said.

"What is it?" Irwin turned to give Caitlin his full attention.

"The child is very intelligent. But also nefarious."

"Yes, I've heard that from her psychiatrist," Irwin said.

"You didn't warn me," Caitlin said.

"Everyone should make up their own mind about a person. It's not good practice to pass along someone else's judgment."

"In this case, it would have helped me if you'd issued a warning. Then I would have had Dr. Polly sit with me and help me as I interviewed the eyewitness."

"We can't pay Dr. Polly to sit with you. That's not part of the department's budget. You're the top forensic artist in the country. You're telling me you've never worked with a difficult eyewitness?"

"Well, yes, I have—"

"Then go to work. Be finished by Wednesday," Irwin said, turning his back on her.

Caitlin felt rebuffed and unsettled by this treatment. Plenty of people at NYPD assigned difficult jobs, but they give you full information first. This must be a Southern California thing, this omission of information mixed with deep hostility couched in soft, flaky, passive-aggressive behavior. Caitlin didn't like Irwin Sanchez much, she decided right there. Irwin must have sensed his popularity waning. As Caitlin gathered her things to leave his office, Irwin called out after her, "After you're done with the sketch, I'll take you to Santa Monica Pier. You can't spend a week at the beach and not ride the roller coaster . . ."

-

Caitlin found Cecily playing a video game on her iPad. It was the hottest part of the afternoon, it could have been 100 degrees, and Cecily was splayed out on a chaise chair with her face, chest, and legs burning. Her skin was blistering red.

"Let's try this again. There's some shade under this umbrella, and this is where I'm going to set up my easel. I'd like you to pull that chair next to me, and give me a few words, images, memories from Monday night. Can you do that?" Caitlin asked.

"Did you bring what I asked for?" Cecily called back, not looking up from her iPad. A casino tune hummed from a vent on the side of the iPad.

"I did. I brought what you asked," Caitlin said.

Cecily dropped the iPad into the grass. She strolled over to where Caitlin's easel was parked. Caitlin handed her a plastic sleeve of Oreos.

"Can we begin again? Can I ask you a few questions?" Caitlin asked, picking up a set of special Italian colored pencils.

"I don't care what you do," Cecily answered, smashing black-and-white cookies between her teeth. Caitlin watched as the girl ingested two, three, four cookies at a time. The corners of Cecily's mouth grew black with Oreo dust. "Actually, I do care. I changed my mind. I do care. I want you to tell all those people in the house to leave. Then I want you to come inside so I can show you something in the kitchen."

Caitlin said, "Those people in the kitchen are solving the murder. You should be grateful that so many people are working so hard to find out who invaded your house on Monday night and caused this terrible thing to happen."

"I want them to leave," Cecily said. "Then I'll do your drawing."

For the next hour, Caitlin tried several techniques. She used special flashcards that she'd designed in a Quantico lab. The cards displayed facial features—noses, chins, eyes, lips, jawlines, hairstyles—for the express purpose of helping children describe things for which they had no adjectives. She discovered that Cecily knew all the adjectives but lost interest too quickly to put a face together. As soon as Caitlin made progress—height, hair color, or nose shape—Cecily would practice cartwheels.

"Look at me! Look at me!" Cecily cried out, her legs in the air. She wheeled herself over a chaise chair, the dress twisted around her waist revealing stained, blue underwear. Her gangly legs twisted, flew, and smacked the pole of an umbrella. Her knee went *thwack*.

"Stop that now," Caitlin cried out harshly.

Now Cecily held her knee, sobbing.

"Please stop that," Caitlin said again, but the more that Caitlin tried to quiet her, the more Cecily erupted into violent wailing. Her cheeks grew purple. Eventually, Cecily's sobbing and crying and wailing was so loud, so intrusive, that several CSIs emerged.

"What's going on out here?" one CSI asked, with concern.

Now Caitlin grew beet-red, frustrated, and threw down her flashcards. Noses, chins, eyes, lips, jawlines, hairstyles scattered onto the grass. She stood, took her bag from where it hung on the corner of a chair, tried to compose herself. She brushed past a CSI on her way out.

"In all my years . . ." Caitlin said with exasperation.

Cecily understood that her antics had caused the end of Caitlin's workday, and all at once she became delighted. Her sobbing turned to high-pitched laughing. She was howling, shouting, giggling, turning somersaults in the grass. She screeched at Caitlin, who had walked away in frustration and was pulling open the doors to the kitchen. "I stole your phone! I stole your phone! You can't go anywhere because I stole your phone!"

-

That night, Caitlin tossed and turned in bed. She barely slept. She had nightmare upon nightmare. When the sun rose, she peered out her window at the butter-yellow stucco walls. Then she padded to the bathroom and sat in the window seat, combed her silver-white hair into a bob, clipped it with a tortoiseshell clip, dabbed petroleum on the pads of her eyes and checked her nails and teeth for decay. She went to the kitchen in her grey sweater set and grey slacks and grey windbreaker, started the coffee maker, burned the toast, and thought, *I can do this. Today will be better.*

When she passed the jacaranda tree on her way out, she noticed its fruit had fallen overnight. Now there were big red splotches on the outdoor stairs. The smashed fruit gave off a stench. Inside the Big Blue Bus, she felt depressed. The palm trees looked dry and cracked and brown. The cement looked bleached-out. The runners and bikers seemed aggressive today, cutting across the road when they didn't have the right-of-way.

"I can't finish a portrait by Wednesday," Caitlin told Irwin. "This girl won't give me one inch of description. She refuses to remember anything from Monday night. She asks me for favors all day long. I submit to her, and she gives nothing back. Yesterday I unearthed her iPad from her disaster zone of a room, I bought her a package of Oreos, I bought her a frozen slushy drink from Starbucks, and what happened? What was the result of all this? She grew lazy and recalcitrant. Then she tried to manipulate me into doing evil things. I have a feeling, an instinct, that the girl is seriously deranged, and the mother was under duress. Maybe the mother asked someone for help, and maybe the event unfolded from there. Have you considered this possibility? Either way, I can't finish a portrait of a suspect without a *single word of description* from the eyewitness. I certainly can't do it by Wednesday," Caitlin said.

Irwin paused, considered how to respond. "The manny said the same thing."

"The manny?" Caitlin asked.

"The girl had a manny. A male nanny who quit a year ago," Irwin said. "He said it was the most dysfunctional house he'd ever worked in. The girl was a tyrant. An absolute monster. He felt unsafe in her presence. When we called to interview him, to ask for his help on behalf of the family, he said they can go to hell."

"You didn't think to tell me this before?" Caitlin asked.

-

"Cecily, I'm going to try once more, then I'm leaving," Caitlin called out. "Will you please sit next to me at the table and focus? Answer my list of questions?"

Today, Cecily was in a red polka-dot bikini. It was 9 a.m. and she was in the shallow end of the pool playing a video game on her iPad. With the other hand, she gripped an ice cream cone with a scoop of chocolate ice cream. The sun beat down on the tiles of the pool, the heat was already oppressive, and the ice cream cone was fast turning to soup. It melted, *drip drop drip drop*, down Cecily's forearm and into the turquoise water.

"Mrs. Caitlin Rex. I'll do that after you play my game!" Cecily called out.

"I'll consider it today. Because certainly nothing else has worked out. But I've noticed a pattern with you. I do whatever you ask me to do, and you never pay me back with your cooperation. It doesn't matter how many favors I do for you, when it's time for you to sit and listen and answer questions, when it's time to make a sketch of the suspect, you refuse to help," Caitlin answered.

"I *will* cooperate this time. I promise I will," Cecily whined.

Caitlin couldn't put her finger on it, maybe it was wishful thinking, but the girl seemed ready to work with her today. Plus,

Cecily's wet curls were stuck to her forehead, her tiny ribcage protruded from the bikini, her bird shoulders were stooped forward, and altogether, she looked weak, pathetic, and sad.

"Okay, Cecily," Caitlin said. "Let's make a deal. I'll do whatever you ask me to do, so long as you help me finish at least one draft, a sketch of the suspect. Okay?"

Cecily gazed up with demonic eyes.

-

The kitchen was deserted. The CSIs had gone down to the police station for a big meeting, so everything was carefully laid out, preserved, and labelled. Cecily tore through the place in her polka-dot bikini, dripping pool water onto the Spanish tiles.

"Where are you?" Caitlin asked.

"Keep your eyes closed. Keep the blindfold on—" Cecily told Caitlin.

Caitlin had studied the kitchen enough times now to know that she was near the oven, at the wall that divides the pantry.

"Where do you want me to stand?" Caitlin asked.

"Right there—" Cecily said. She scurried back and forth. Caitlin didn't know what Cecily was doing, but she heard a long, inflexible thing, like a cord being dragged somewhere. She heard Cecily fiddling, moving something.

"Don't move anything, Cecily—" Caitlin warned.

"I'm not! I'm not moving anything! But you need to inch this way." Cecily then clasped her hands on Caitlin's hips. She whispered into her ear, "Okay. Bend down."

Caitlin let the girl guide her hand lower, toward the floor. Cecily tugged hard at her arm. "Cecily, I don't like this—" she said.

At the last minute, she recoiled, pulled back, but it was too late. The whirr of the twelve-pound blender filled the air. The blindfold was off. She watched her fourth finger and pinky finger swirl into the metal blades. Cecily shrieked and laughed, as the blood splattered against the oven.

-

"What happened to you?" the bus driver asked when she climbed on the Big Blue Bus the next morning. Caitlin refused to answer. She was in no mood. She'd spent the whole night in the emergency room. She'd managed only an hour of work, but she was determined to deliver this portrait. With her right hand bandaged up in a plaster cast and sling, she made her way to the Santa Monica police station.

Today she wore her gold cross necklace, the one her husband gave her for their twenty-fifth anniversary. She held it to her chest with her left hand, as she watched the bus veer off its normal path. Today, they went along the boardwalk. The sun looked black. The beach was trash-strewn, with dispossessed people, ghouls, lying about.

"Here's the sketch you asked for." Caitlin dropped it on Irwin's desk.

Irwin was so shocked to see her that he didn't know what to say. He wore a dumb look of surprise, like he was responsible for everything but not responsible for anything. He certainly wasn't expecting Mrs. Caitlin Rex to show up to work. But now he saw why she did. There on his desk was a strangely perfect portrait—strange because it was done with Caitlin's left hand, not her right—of Cecily's big, tear-stained, blue eyes.

"Are you sure?" Irwin asked her.

Caitlin took her leather bag, bulging with items, and headed into the hallway. She heard Irwin call out behind her, "Can we call you for a job next month?"

Chapter Two. Bitcoin Dreams

November 2022. Moulin Hotel Club in Miami, Florida. I walked in as a bathtub of stale champagne was being carried out by workers. The neon lights were blazing on a troupe of trapeze dancers who'd been working all night. One trapeze dancer was entertaining herself, cartwheeling on a high rope in sequined bra and tights while her friend was being interviewed by a detective. Behind that detective, several cops roamed the 3,000-square-foot nightclub, shining their flashlights under blood-red velvet divans, cordoning off areas with yellow tape. One cop was lifting magnums of Domaines Ott Rosé, checking their bottoms. The mood was casual and untroubled. Someone had called in a noise disturbance. Because Moulin Hotel Club was the newest, poshest, most secretive club trafficked by the rich and discreet, the Miami Police Department was curious to get inside.

I flashed my credentials. I tried to move past a senior detective. I asked him politely if he could step out of the way.

"Ma'am. Who are *you?*" he asked sharply.

I turned my head to avoid his direct stare. *You stupid idiot,* I berated myself. *You're a thirty-nine-year-old woman standing here in blond hair extensions, high heels, a trench-coat uniform. If he starts asking questions, he'll know you don't belong here. The badge is a fake. He doesn't even know Frank Keenan is hiding upstairs.*

"Sorry, I didn't mean to bother you," I said quickly.

Then I held my breath and prayed. While the detective turned his back and talked to someone else, I slipped past him. I went through the black lacquered doors with oval windows that led to the kitchen behind the dance floor. In the kitchen, I strolled by stainless-steel appliances, through another door into a plush, carpeted hallway. It was quiet back here. Framed black-and-white photos of Hollywood stars from the 1920s led the way upstairs. I knocked on the door marked EXECUTIVE SUITE.

"Hey, Frank, it's me—" I whispered. "Can you let me in? The police are downstairs."

The shadow of two feet approached the door sill. There was heavy breathing followed by sharp whimpers. *Uh oh,* I thought. *Frank is not doing well. His breathing is ragged.* Between breaths, I heard him sob. "Frank, are you okay?"

The door to the office cracked open.

Frank Keenan stood there, his eyes bulging yellow and full of gunk. His lips were swollen and bruised. He'd been beaten up badly. He was shaking. In his crumpled velvet blazer, khakis, diving watch, white powder and dried blood stuck to one nostril—he cut an expensive, deranged, and disheveled figure.

"Why didn't you answer your phone?" he whispered, bolting the door.

I looked around. Nothing was out of place. Not a single hair on the pale carpet. The executive office of this club, where something had gone terribly wrong, was immaculate. The sitting area, with its Eames furniture and cream pillows with pale brown piping, looked inviting. The coffee table books were lined up squarely on the pale wood table. Through the pale wood-encased windows I could see wraparound views of a turquoise Miami Bay. The bay was surreal, peaceful, and quiet. Picnic boats bobbed in the distance.

"THIS IS ALL YOUR FUCKING FAULT!" Frank exploded. "Why didn't you pick up your phone when I called you?"

"What? No. What are you talking about? You left me a message at 3:40 this morning that I couldn't understand. I called you back. Then I received all these SOS texts . . ."

I held up my phone to show him my outgoing call.

"ALL OF THIS! IT'S YOUR FUCKING FAULT!" he erupted again. His shoulders shook with rage. His black curls, laced with grey, convulsed. His knees buckled and bent before he collapsed to the carpet. I watched him and thought, *Maybe he's having a drug seizure. He hasn't slept in a week. Someone slipped him a bad pill.*

Frank crawled to me on all fours. In turns of mania he groped my knees, gurgled air, and shouted up at me. "YOU TOLD ME! YOU SAID YOU'D PROTECT ME!!!! THAT MAN IS A LUNATIC. HE THREATENED TO CUT OUT MY KIDNEY!!! OVER BITCOIN! OVER FORTY BITCOIN!!! HE IS A DERANGED LUNATIC!"

"Lower your voice," I said. "The police are downstairs. If they see you like this, they'll arrest you and I can't protect you."

"YOU DIDN'T PROTECT ME!!!" Frank exploded.

He started rocking, shaking, chewing his lip, moaning from the depths of his stomach. *"You…you liar…" "You lied to me…" "You knew you were lying to me…" "How could you do this to me?" "You fucked me…all my work…" "I'm ruined…"*

Frank was in the fetal position now. While he shed bloody snot, drool, and tears down the front of his shirt, I shut my eyes. I felt pressure building in my skull. Pressure. Intense, blinding, white-hot pressure. Like a hammer between the eyes, it hit me that I was implicated in this mess. There was no way out of this unless I somehow left, escaped, without anyone knowing I'd ever talked to Frank Keenan. But there was the transcript. There were several copies of the transcript. The weekend-long interview I'd conducted. At least four people in Washington, D.C., *knew* that I was in the know. And here was Frank Keenan. Falling apart.

Several voices sounded in the hallway. It was the cops.

"Frank. Whatever your boss said to you, whatever he did, you need to tell me right now before the Miami police walk through that door."

But Frank couldn't speak. His eyes were closed. He jutted his hand toward the area behind the couch. That's when I saw it. A shoe, the tip of a brown loafer peeking out. *Please God, tell me this isn't what I think it is...*

The cops were trying the door handle. Banging lightly at the door. I felt my heartbeat through my shirt as I approached the sofa and looked behind it.

"*You...said you'd protect me...you cunt...*" Frank sobbed.

-

Before there was FTX, the Bitcoin debacle that everyone in the world knows about, there was GXU. In fact, the primary reason that I, Daisy Renfrew—I'll say my name now—missed the white smoke, red flags, and warning signals that FTX sent up before its $32.5 billion implosion, one critical explanation, one excuse, apology, pretext, plea, ploy, defense—whatever you want to label it—is that my team, my committee, my basketball squad of regulators (formed between the cracks of six major U.S. legal and regulatory and spy agencies) was dealing with an uglier mess. That mess was the broker-dealer

GXU, or as known by its hedge fund arm, GXU Capital. Why did we choose GXU? Because Lai Yang, the founder of GXU was making more money than any person on earth. *Get ahead of this,* the senator told me.

I was the woman in charge of providing answers.

A committee was formed to study centralized payment systems, cryptocurrency, and blockchain. The committee was organized and funded by a top dog in Senate. The elected official wanted to know what feast of indiscretion was being enjoyed, but he also *didn't* want to know. So it was, my first instruction was to be discreet.

So much for that.

November of 2022, before the bottom fell out, I went to visit Frank Keenan at a cut-rate casino motel on the border of New York and Canada. At that time, you'll learn, Frank Keenan wanted out of GXU. He wanted nothing to do with his company anymore. What happened instead is that we forced him to stay inside. In a nonchalant, bureaucratic way, we threatened him within an inch of his life. "If you don't feed us a steady drip of information on Lai Yang and his company and the atrocities being committed therein, we will show you a very special door to hell." In exchange for his services, we promised we'd protect him.

So it was, GXU was in our crosshairs. Frank, our insider-turned-whistleblower, went back to work for GXU where he posed as a loyal, dedicated employee. My committee received an IV tube of inside information. Things went well until they didn't.

A year into the project, my committee, my squad of black-belt regulators was getting ready to present our final report to the Commission. We were getting ready to shutter the doors at GXU when from under the palm trees on a Bahamian Island, another founder, one we hadn't been looking at all— Sam Bankman-Fried from FTX—told the world via tweet that he had "plenty of liquidity." Just as chaos in the world broke out, chaos in my personal life broke out. I learned that Frank Keenan was trapped at the Moulin Hotel Club in Miami. His boss, Lai Yang, had committed a series of crimes I could barely type in an e-mail. Now I had to get to Miami, silence our witness, and find every copy of the interview transcript from the weekend I spent with Frank Keenan.

One copy remains. It is contained below.

-

Early December 2021. From Washington, D.C., I flew to JFK, and from JFK I drove to Buffalo. I arrived at the Executive Stay & Play Casino Suites thirty miles from the Canadian border in a snowstorm. The parking lot was full of salt-crusted minivans and shuttlebuses. People from all walks of life were trudging snow and ice from the soles of their boots onto the red carpet in the lobby. The heat was pumping full blast from the ceiling vents, pushing a row of dusty, fake, palm trees sideways. I could hear slot machines ringing in the vestibule, just beyond the front desk. I stood waiting for the manager to find the keys to the room I'd booked. He finally said there was no room available now. This was a popular weekend. He instructed me to walk around the place, amuse myself, and come back when a room was available. My phone buzzed. (The following is the transcript from the interview I conducted over forty-eight hours. Sections appear in my report to the Commission.)

Keenan: Are you here?

Me: I got here half an hour ago. I've already lost at blackjack.

Keenan: Why don't you come up to my room and we'll get started?

Me: What room are you in?

Keenan: Room 422.

Me: How the hell did you choose this place?

Keenan: I needed somewhere to hide. This fit the bill.

The man I was there to meet, Frank Keenan, was holed up at the Executive Stay & Play Casino Suites. He was fifty-something, a widower with grown daughters. He was six feet tall and in prime condition, with the kind of excess brawn that would deter most people from picking a fight. Tidy black curls and a groomed beard. His nose was big but not unhandsome. Later, he told me he was Brooklyn-born Irish, Irish all the way back, but you'd never guess it from his olive skin. He was nearsighted. But his eyesight problems were variable. When he answered the door, he removed his thin wire frames. To study my face, he put his glasses on. To show me around the hotel suite, he took the glasses off. Also, he kept licorice in his pocket. I later found out it was caffeinated licorice.

Me: So, this your hideout?

Keenan: It's the headquarters for my investigation.

Me: Your investigation or your defense?

Keenan: It's a good question. I'll guess we'll know in a few months when the world figures out what's going on at my company.

Me: You're the chief economist at GXU?

Keenan: For three years and three days. Lai Yang and his business, GXU, were a puzzle to me when I joined. I didn't know how he was making so much money from a small Bitcoin broker dealer—the volume of trades wasn't initially large. But credible, qualified people at the University of Chicago and in Silicon Valley told me to take the job. I wish I hadn't.

Me: I'm sure.

Keenan: Look around while I decide where to start.

Frank has converted this two-bedroom suite into an investigation of what GXU is *actually* doing in global Bitcoin markets. It's an activity which by his admission has taken him months. "I might only be in the third inning—" he remarked. "Yes, I'm chief economist, but no one, I mean *no one*, has a clear handle on the sedition that runs through the heart of this company." As chief economist, Frank has a senior, coveted position in the company. He holds a board position. In some ways, he's the right hand of the king. Lai Yang trusts him. So Frank has access to plenty of information. Other information, Frank pointed out, he's had to "beg, borrow and steal."[2]

The hotel suite appears clean, if wholly cluttered. The place reminds me of a scene from *All the President's Men*. The volume of material is overwhelming. What isn't taped or tacked or pinned to the wall is piled high in paper stacks, on every surface including the window ledge. Printouts—thousands of pieces of paper—show wire transfers and trade confirms, WhatsApp messages, voicemails, Reuters and Bloomberg messages, payment app instructions, numerical codes, tweets, trade confirmations, settlement instructions, broker and exchange confirmations, e-mails, pin codes, unwind instructions, Snapchat messages and Instagram DMs, back-to-back authorizations, bank statements, bank names, bank subsidiary names, bank custodial names, bank routing numbers and SWIFT numbers, bank locations on maps, London, Zurich, Hong Kong, Johannesburg, Singapore, Frankfurt, Chicago, Moscow, Miami, New York, New York, New York, Palo Alto, London and Johannesburg again, Melbourne, Sidney, Istanbul, Brussels, Isle of Man, Cayman Islands, Nassau, Miami, New York.

---

2 This interview with Frank Keenan is also contained in audio transcript. Various comments, footnoted, were recorded by hand.

Across one wall there's a giant plastic atlas with different colored push tacks. The push tacks are connected to threads of corresponding color, red, blue, neon yellow, neon orange, green, purple, etc. The thread is strung around the world from pin to pin, explaining how payments move—Bitcoin, cash, gold, other tokens—Litecoin, stablecoins, Dogecoin, Tether, Ethereum, FTT coin. Bank to bank. Legal entity to legal entity. There's a key on the side that denotes the temporal natures of these flows. TIME is stamped in bold next to columns of dates: Q1 2018; Q2 2018; Q4 2018; Q2 2019; Q3 2019; and so on. Dollar notional amounts are clarified on a second corresponding chart: $70.2 million; $2.25 million; $635,555; $10.65 million; $175.3257 million; $5.05 million; etc. Next to this giant morass, along a wall of windows, taped to the slat blinds, are press clippings, headlines, and bios of every employee at GXU. A huge photograph, a headshot, is stuck to the center of the window. This is a photograph of Lai Yang. I recognize the face immediately.

Me: Where do you sleep?

Frank: I sleep in the other room. Do you want to see it?

I wander into the second, connecting room. This is where Frank has made his living quarters. A queen bed with a rumpled red and brown striped coverlet, a closet with several oxford shirts hanging, a wet blue towel hung on the corner of the bathroom door. A hunk of shaving cream stuck to the towel. The bathmat in a ball in front of the sink. Two framed photographs of Frank's grown daughters, propped on the bedside stand. A plastic iced-coffee cup filled with water. A small, low bookshelf next to the bed. Frank's personal book collection. His taste skews toward gonzo journalism. Beat literature. Ginsberg, Burroughs, Kerouac, Thompson, Kesey, Wolfe. Plus, the seminal works of Adam Smith and Karl Marx. Two more by the financial historian John Kenneth Galbraith.

Me: Why did no one see the scandal brewing at GXU?

Keenan: There are so many reasons.

Me: Give me one.

Keenan: It's a jigsaw puzzle that requires intense focus to put together. If you had any idea how many hours it's taken me to dive into this, to untangle the legitimate business from the illegitimate business, to *find* the first fraudulent cash flow and connect it to the second and third fraudulent cash flow and then connect it to a pattern—to follow that pattern of fraud—if you had any idea how many times I had to go back and forth in time, location, method, motive, language, currency translation—I had to travel from New York to Zurich and back to New York in a single day to convince two banks to physically agree on wire evidence—if you had any idea how difficult this jigsaw puzzle of an investigation is, you'd get back in your car and drive home.

Me: I might do that anyway. If I can't get a room.

Keenan: You can sleep on that couch. It's a pull-out.

Me: That's not appealing.

We go back in the first room, and my eyes fall on the thousands upon thousands of printouts, information, diligence I'll need to study, consume, copy, verify, incorporate into my report. The overwhelm clouds my eyes. Frank pats my shoulder. He sits in a pretzel position on the floor, amidst documents, and scratches his back using the couch leg.

Keenan: It comes down to a single trade. My boss, Lai Yang, fabricated the first series of trades, and from there, it spirals out.

Me: I have a stupid question.

Keenan: Go for it.

Me: You've managed to collect all this without anyone at GXU knowing?

Keenan: Yes.

Me: Where do they think you are right now?

Keenan: Lecturing. Abroad.

Me: One more stupid question.

Keenan: Go for it.

Me: In your e-mail you called GXU a "Headless Ponzi Scheme." Is that a technical term?

Keenan: Yes and no.

Me: Because on Monday, I need to fly to Washington, D.C., and report to the Commission. Joint Task Force Committee. What I'd like is the facts. Just the facts. I don't want a side of the story that absolves you from the mess. I don't want your guesstimates. If I spend an entire weekend at a cut-rate casino in Buffalo, and if at the end of this, I have nothing, if I end up telling a room full of bureaucrats that my only explanation is that there is no explanation, I'll be an unhappy woman.

Keenan: Let's start at the beginning.

Me: Good.

Keenan: I have one request.

Me: Lay it on me.

Keenan: When the time comes, you will help me flee the country.

Me: What?

-

In Frank Keenan's defense, late in 2019 he sent a shot across the bow. He sent an e-mail to a friend named W. at the Securities and Exchange Commission. The e-mail was alarming. Frank told the regulatory agency he had "serious moral qualms" about the way his company was presenting itself to investors. He *all but specified* that the SEC or CFTC, some regulatory body somewhere, should investigate claims that GXU was making to investors. Via social media advertisements and TV advertisements, a GXU fund had listed returns from its black box product. The black box product wasn't labeled "yield farming"—that term would come later—but that's essentially what it was. GXU was guaranteeing twelve-percent-plus returns, without saying how those returns were generated. The Sharpe ratio, the risk-adjusted performance of the black box product, was abnormally high. Frank said his friend W. printed out his warning e-mail and took in into the office of the man who at that time ran the SEC. The head of the SEC was a man who came out of the Chicago pits, where his father had traded pork bellies in the '70s, and he'd traded lumber, gold, silver, oil, natural gas—real things only, during the '90s and '00s. He was allergic to all things Bitcoin-related. He hated every human involved in Bitcoin. When W. presented Frank's e-mail, the head of the SEC read it carefully. Then he tore the printout into tiny pieces which he stuffed in the shredder under his desk. The shredder made a low, churning hum as it ate the paper. The head of the SEC said, "I hate those freaks."

-

Keenan: Lai Yang. Let's start with him.

Frank nods at the sepia photograph, the headshot taped to the slat blinds. It shows a forty-something man, American, with dark fluffy hair and a gap in his teeth. Spread-out eyes. Chin dimple. There's a pleasing quality, a spaciousness to the man's facial features. You can see how investors like and trust him. It's only a headshot, so I can't fully see what Lai Yang is wearing below his white oxford shirt and recognizable Brooks Brothers tie pattern. Scrawled on his forehead in sharpie marker is his name: **Lai Yang**.

Me: When was this picture taken?

Keenan: Around the time he hired me to GXU. That was Q3 2017.

Me: You were teaching at the University of Chicago then?

Keenan: I was about to leave academia. As Kissinger said, the problem with academia is that the people are poisonous and the stakes pitifully low. I'm paraphrasing here, but you get it.

I couldn't see a future writing research that no one reads. I just couldn't see it. I was living in Lincoln Park, going through an expensive divorce, so I couldn't leave the University of Chicago paycheck and benefits behind. Not without something else in the pipeline. I applied to be a research strategist for a well-known German bank, and I got the offer. The salary was okay, but the bank was under ECB scrutiny. Bonuses just weren't being paid. The benefits were fine. Anyway, I declined. I applied for another job. Whatever. It's not interesting. The point is, I was just hanging out at the University of Chicago, kind of half in, half out, showing up but not putting in effort. You know what I mean?

Me: I do.

Keenan: One day, and I swear to God this is how it happened, I was standing in my kitchen in my jogging clothes. I was about to go for a jog. My next-door neighbor, this ninety-year-old Chinese woman who wears bedroom slippers and drives a white Mercedes, knocked on my door. She was having car trouble. She asked for help. I don't know anything about her but she's as nice as can be. I go outside to help her. We go to her driveway and there's her car. She left it on, running. She tells me she can't move the car forward because there's this crazy little mouse running around in circles. Blocking her way. I go look. There it is. This tiny mouse running in tight circles right under the front fender of her Mercedes. It's amazing she saw it. The old lady asks me if I can move the mouse, and then she gets a plastic shopping bag from her trunk. She gives me a bag so I can trap the mouse. I bend down to get the mouse, at which point I hear yapping. Insane yapping. The lady has a litter of dogs—three or four little fluffy caramel things—locked in the car. They can smell the mouse. Every time they yap, yap, yap, yap, yap, the lady is getting upset.

Me: Go on.

Keenan: So, I get the mouse in the shopping bag, I follow the lady up her driveway to her house, which is this massive Greek neo-classical thing with the curtains sealed shut. I'm standing there. Wondering what she wants me to do next. The old lady starts crying. She apologizes. The she cries again. She tells me her son just started a very big investment fund and has become very rich. I can't figure out why she's crying. Then she tells me she's upset because he moved to Palo Alto to base his fund and recruit talent. Palo Alto is all the way across the country, and the lady tells me she doesn't have the energy to fly. She hates the airports. Anyway, eventually we get to his name, Lai Yang, and I'm thinking, this can't be the same Lai Yang who I just read about in *Wired* magazine. I'm thinking, this can't be the Lai Yang who ran a huge fund at Sentry Asset Management in Valley Forge, Pennsylvania. There's no way. But then she goes on about him, and I realize, *it is the same guy.* We get talking. I tell her, I'm a University of Chicago economist looking for a gig. We go inside her house, and she calls him on the phone. She calls Lai Yang, right there on the spot.

Me: And he hires you?

Keenan: He hired me. I flew out the next day.

Me: Can I ask what he offered you in salary and bonus?

Keenan: Four times my 2017 compensation, plus moving expenses, plus carry in several different GXU sub-funds, plus an interest in GXU Capital. When I added it up it was more than I'd ever made in my life.

Me: You couldn't say no to the job.

Keenan: I couldn't say no to the job.

Me: Was your antenna up? I mean, typically, when financial employers of the highest reputation hire they don't *need* to pay so much. Part of the compensation is their reputation they lend to you. For instance, Goldman Sachs offers less in salary and bonuses to new employees than, say, a bank of lesser reputation.

Keenan: Okay sure. But this is Bitcoin. This is cryptocurrency. You're looking at banks, traditional finance, as your model for how things work. Bitcoin straddles several worlds; finance but also technology and venture capital and private equity and then all the dark arts, like gaming and meme stock trading. I mean, when Lai Yang hired me for GXU, he needed an economist of some reputation, but the pay package was designed to be competitive so that I wouldn't be hired to another Bitcoin fund. Bitcoin funds draw talent from this other world. The compensation packages reflect that. It's a whole different thing.

Me: Okay, I'm just looking for red flags.

Keenan: I get it. But I wasn't suspicious when I first started working at GXU. Look at Lai Yang in 2018. Lai Yang was doing everything right, everything aboveboard. Remember, he'd earned as sterling a reputation as anyone could earn. Just look at him. Lai Yang wore Brooks Brothers ties and had a blue-blood résumé. Deerfield Academy, Harvard University, Wharton Business School, Sentry Asset Management. The guy was a member of several golf clubs, like

Liberty National and Bayonne in New Jersey. He wanted to get into Augusta National or Pine Valley, but he had miles ahead of him. He came from nowhere. He was a socially awkward nerd. His wife, for heaven's sakes, was an advisory project manager at Deloitte. He was a devoted husband. Mama's boy. It broke his heart to move across the country away from his mom. This was an upstanding guy who'd worked his fingers to the bone. He'd done *everything* by the book. His life was built for a résumé. He never broke a rule. He didn't have a speeding ticket. That was Lai Yang.

Me: Okay, let's fast-forward to the illegal part.

Keenan: Wait, first I want to talk about Lai Yang and his vision for GXU. If you understand the man and the vision, how committed he was to the vision, you'll see how messed up things became.

Me: Fine. Go ahead.

Keenan: So, before Lai Yang came along, there was this idea out there that anyone who sold Bitcoin or Bitcoin trading services was selling snake oil.

Me: I still have that idea.

Keenan: Lai Yang wanted to improve the reputation of Bitcoin and the cryptocurrency universe in total. He wanted to study the four categories of risk: suitability of investment for the consumer, information presented to the consumer via the prospectus, infrastructure and operational concerns. He wanted to improve, you know, how cryptocurrency assets are traded, the size of transaction, the speed of transaction, the bid-offer spread. Lastly, he wanted to improve legal protections. He was *against* fraud.

Me: How was he going to accomplish his vision?

Keenan: By building the best Bitcoin exchange on the planet. GXU was designed to be a marketplace where buyers and sellers could meet, trust one another, and trust the technology. It was about trust. That may sound simple, but until GXU, there was no such thing.

Me: Great. Skip to the illegal part.

Keenan: Well. So, 2019 started well for GXU. Recall GXU was a plain vanilla business.

It was a traditional exchange, a broker-dealer, to facilitate Bitcoin trading. Originally, Lai Yang wanted it to serve *only* qualified investors who *only* wanted to trade Bitcoin. GXU would collect a fee for each transaction, just like Schwab or Ameritrade does. As the profit model evolved, as he raised more money to fund hockey-stick projections, Lai Yang learned how limiting his original vision was. He expanded the vision. He widened his customer base. He widened his product offering. By 2019, all cryptocurrency, every token held in every dark market in the world, some with zero reputation, zero volume, zero liquidity, were listed on our drop-down menu of "tradable products." Any customer who logged onto GXU's broker-dealer platform could see that we'd make a market *in anything*. I mean, let's say you were a cryptocurrency trader living in Egypt. You mint a coin called Pyramid Coin—I'm making this up, giving you an example—and suddenly you want liquidity for all this coin you designed. If you're a customer of GXU, you can log onto the GXU platform and just list your amount of Pyramid Coin for offer, with a little description beneath of who trades it, why it's valuable, etc. You can set up several trading entities that trade Pyramid Coin back and forth, at whatever price they settle on. Red Dragon wants to buy 1 Pyramid Coin for 70 Swiss francs? Blue Box is willing to sell at 1 Pyramid Coin for 70 Swiss francs. GXU is happy to facilitate the transaction, collect a fee on that transaction, because that's the business model of GXU.

Me: Okay. And?

Keenan: Well, think about it. Some trader sitting in Egypt just made up a claim. Then he made up two entities to trade the claim, attaching some arbitrary value, and GXU's business is to *legitimize* the transaction by saying, yes, thank you, we'll collect a fee on this transaction. We'll record it on our books. We'll show it to a *legitimate* New York or Silicon Valley private equity fund who wants to invest money in our broker-dealer platform, to show them just how much trading volume there is on our platform. Endless trading volume! Endless demand! Forget the fact that Pyramid Coin is worth nothing. Red Dragon is a fictitious entity, Blue Box is a fictitious entity, and 70 Swiss francs was a price pulled out of the sky.

Me: Let me stop you right there.

Keenan: Fine. Go ahead.

Me: GXU's Bitcoin trading business *was* legitimate. People buy and sell lots of Bitcoin. Bitcoin has a verifiable price history. Deep liquidity. Massive trading volumes. The profits that GXU booked for several quarters were real.

Keenan: Sure, yes, and you could say the same thing about Enron's gas trading business. It *was* legitimate. But then there were other things. Other activities that led Enron out of the Garden of Eden. The same thing applies here. If Lai Yang had stuck to his original business model, where GXU *only* served qualified investors who *only* traded Bitcoin, if Lai Yang had been content to collect a fee on these transactions and no others, all would be well. I wouldn't be holed up in a casino motel trying to avoid being dragged to white-collar jail, and you wouldn't be sitting here interviewing me. By the way, are you hungry?

Me: Famished.

Keenan: Let's talk over dinner.

We go downstairs to the steakhouse. It's a dump. We choose a stained, turquoise-velvet booth with a view of the casino. The table hasn't been cleared. There's a chewed-up steak and cold fries staring me in the face as I sit down. More food is smashed into the rose pattern in the carpet that goes wall-to-wall in this restaurant. When the waitress appears, she has pits stains on her silk blouse. Her bangs are matted to her forehead. Her pupils are as wide as night. She hands us menus, tries to clear the table, and breaks two martini glasses in the process. Now there's glass shards everywhere. I stand up again to walk away, to give this scene wide berth. I go to the entrance and take in a group of college-age men, human wreckage, placing bets at the craps table. Drunk. High. Sweaty. Farting.

Me: I don't know if I can spend the weekend here.

Keenan: You have something against Upstate New York?

Me: Yes. Upstate New York is the pits. I can say that, by the way, because my family is from here. I'm from here.

Keenan: Where?

Me: Ithaca.

Keenan: I gave a lecture at Cornell in 2020, and a Nobel-prize economist congratulated me on taking a job at GXU. He told me I was working on the frontier of human possibility. He used those words.

Me: Did he know GXU was a "Headless Ponzi Scheme"?

Keenan: Okay, so let's get back to that. As I said, 2019 started well. GXU wasn't doing anything illegal. I have thousands of hours of research to prove that point. Lai Yang was raising money at bigger and bigger valuations, and the growth rate of that valuation was higher than any growth rate of any competitor in the world. Lai Yang pointed to the second derivative, the growth rate of his valuation, in every meeting he held. Management meetings. Board meetings.

Meetings with consultants, vendors, big potential institutional customers. Lai Yang was proud of the fact that his *very legitimate* business on the frontier of human possibility—to use the Nobel-prize economist's phraseology—had wide support. I mean, think back to 2019. You were at the Securities & Exchange Commission, and you knew Lai Yang's name, you knew GXU's name. Everyone thought we were the gold standard in cryptocurrency trading.

Me: That's putting words in my mouth.

Keenan: Fine. But we were doing something right.

Me: Go on.

Keenan: Then it went south. The first week of Q2, April it was, Lai Yang was supposed to take vacation with his wife. He hadn't taken a day off in five years. The success, but also the stress, was getting to him. He had stomach cramps. He walked into my office one day and said his intestine was in knots. Lots of trouble sleeping. The pharmacist told him to try a medication called Thorazine. I told him that was crazy. I hadn't heard of anyone taking Thorazine since the '80s. Also, no one takes Thorazine for stomach cramps. There's better stuff out there with negligible side effects. Anyway, his anxiety worsened. His stomach got worse. He must have taken a horse pill of Thorazine. One day he walks into the big glass conference room for our morning meeting—we had a 7 a.m. morning meeting, as is typical in the traditional financial world—we hewed to a lot of traditional practices, by the way—and Lai Yang starts presenting to the group. He's talking about what happened on the overnight bourses, giving a market rundown. Here's how much Japanese yen moved, KGBs sold off, Gold did this, CDX spreads widened, etc., and suddenly, Lai Yang passes out on the carpet. Just hits the deck.

Me: Did he go to the hospital?

Keenan: The paramedics came. The ambulance was there. We *tried* to get him to go to the hospital, get on an IV, get sorted out, but he refused. He just stood up. He went back to his office and sat down in front of his screens. He put through a series of trades around 10 a.m. that morning, and I swear, that's what started everything.

Me: Everything illegal, you mean?

Keenan: Yes. Everything illegal.

Me: Walk me through it.

Keenan: The neon yellow thread on the atlas. Remember it? The morning Lai Yang collapsed, he was trying to solve the problem of how to get a big institutional customer onto his platform. Lai knew that once he convinced one institutional client to use his platform, he'd have them all in his hand. His best shot was Sentry, of course, because he spent the first part of his career *working* for Sentry. They liked him and trusted him. But they didn't trust Bitcoin. They had no plans to trade it. They hated the risk profile of the product, they hated that it was essentially an ungovernable market. Lai Yang had made several trips to Valley Forge to convince them otherwise, but nothing worked. So anyway, he couldn't get Sentry as a customer of GXU but he needed Sentry as a customer of GXU because he'd promised everyone—all his investors, *The Wall Street Journal*—that GXU was going to be the "only" Bitcoin trading platform that would allow big institutional investors to trade safely. He made this promise, he couldn't keep it, and he was growing desperate.

Me: Sounds like Elizabeth Holmes.

Keenan: The history of graft doesn't repeat but it rhymes. Recall Sentry is exactly what its name implies. It's the safest, strongest, most "institutional" of all the mutual funds. Lai Yang was brilliant in his next move. He knew if he could get Sentry's name behind his name, if he could get *them* to use the GXU platform to do business, he could get anyone! Any mutual fund, pension fund, literally every institutional investor would follow suit. But his problem to solve was how to get Sentry to say yes to cryptocurrency. Or more specifically, how could Lai Yang *force* Sentry to do its first cryptocurrency trade? So that's what he did that morning. He solved that little problem with one phone call. Right after he collapsed in the conference room, he went into his office. He called a friend, a portfolio manager at Sentry. I'll leave the guy's name out, but it will come up once they subpoena everything. He said, "If you put through a big trade, say, $250 million notional in Bitcoin using a Sentry block account, if you call your compliance department and *say* you *thought* you had accounts set up between Sentry and GXU, if you do this, I'll make sure you're compensated." Then Lai Yang booked the trade to a block account, which is basically where broker-dealers book trades when they don't have details of a trade. Or a real counterparty.

Me: Is this conjecture? Or you know this happened?

Keenan: I know it happened. He booked the trade illegally.

Me: Do you have evidence?

Keenan: Listen, lady. *The trade went through.* $250 million of Bitcoin was bought by a mutual fund that didn't have Bitcoin in its charter. Do you understand? By Sentry's own rules, *it was illegal* for Sentry to trade Bitcoin. They didn't have accounts on the GXU platform. I have records to prove it. So when Lai Yang put a trade through on Sentry's behalf, when he unilaterally decided to get the oldest investment manager in the U.S. into the riskiest product in the world, it caused a hurricane. A dozen people from the Sentry compliance department were lighting up our phone lines, yelling, "Who booked this?" and "Don't book this trade to us" and "Fix this error" and "This is a mistake!" But Lai Yang stuck to his guns. He said, "No, the trade is good!" Then Lai Yang got on a plane and flew across the country to lobby the powers-that-be at Sentry to let the trade settle. In Valley Forge, he went to war. He engaged in the biggest political campaign of his life. He met every manager at Sentry. He gave assurance after assurance after assurance that the trade was good, the product was good, GXU was a reputable counterparty. It was all about trust. Trust with a capital T. Lai Yang assured them that *until* Sentry compliance officers were comfortable, the trade would sit between two offshore entities. Lai Yang even brought a senator with him! That senator, by the way, is not unbiased. Let's leave it at that. Anyway, Lai Yang offered everything and the kitchen sink to Sentry to approve a trade *they hadn't ordered*. He made sure they were okay with the counterparty risk. With the collateral. With everything. Everything that could be guaranteed was guaranteed and guaranteed again. Forget the fact the guarantees meant nothing. Anyone who trades Bitcoin knows that in less than a second, Bitcoin can trade to zero and no Central Bank in the world will step in to buy. There's *no such thing as a guarantee* in Bitcoin. But Lai Yang, that day, convinced Sentry to sign trading agreements. Sentry started trading.

Me: He booked a fake trade? That's the illegal part?

Keenan: No. That's the tip of the iceberg.

Me: Where's the iceberg?

Keenan: The iceberg is coming. After Lai Yang got Sentry to trade, he got *a dozen* big institutional firms to trade on the GXU platform.

Me: And?

Keenan: And it wasn't enough. It didn't make enough money.

Me: What do you mean?

Keenan: So recall his pie-in-the-sky idea was that once institutional investors were onboarded onto the GXU broker-dealer platform, the trading volumes would be massive. The bid-offer, the fees collected on Bitcoin trading would be so great, that GXU would hit all its financial projections. Exceed them. Investors in GXU would be rewarded and then some. Lai Yang would be on the cover of every fin-tech magazine and the world would be a happier place. That was the pie-in-the-sky idea.

Me: But?

Keenan: But that didn't happen. Sentry started trading. Credit Agricole and Allianz and Pimco, State Street, Alliance Bernstein, Trust Company of the West, whoever, you name it, XYZ big institution set up trading accounts. But they didn't *trade that much.* Even the big fund managers at those firms, the ones who trade everything including Saudi Riyal derivatives, they simply didn't like Bitcoin. So, all these trading agreements were in place. Lai Yang made a carnival show of it in every investor meeting. He went on CNBC and said, "We have *all* the big institutional investors trading Bitcoin on GXU!" But the truth was the volumes were low. Pathetic really. If you looked at the fees collected, the revenue line attached to these customers and their trading activities—it was minimal. There was no revenue. He knew his hockey-stick projections were a hoax. His promise to investors was a lie.

Me: Did he admit this to you? Contemporaneously?

Keenan: No. Founders are like religious leaders. Joseph Smith never whispered into anyone's ear that he *wasn't sure* if the angel landed or *wasn't sure* if that angel handed him those exact gold plates that turned into the Book of Mormon. You know? Lai Yang didn't say he *wasn't sure* about his business model, or that possibly, his business model was a lie of gargantuan proportion. But everyone could see it. GXU wasn't generating revenue.

Me: Can you be specific?

Keenan: Sure. Our valuation dictated that we earn a few hundred million in fees on certain trading days. Some days, we earned a few hundred dollars. Let me repeat that. *A few hundred dollars versus a few hundred million dollars.* By the way, there's this phenomenon called denial. Denial. Denial. Denial. Here's how it works. Everyone claims that money is coming in through the door and that nothing is wrong. If you're an employee of GXU, or an investor, board member, lobbyist, friend, family member, public relations expert, consultant, accountant, website developer, electrician, water or coffee or snacks vendor, graphics designer, insurance salesman—if you sell the company medical, disability, life, title insurance—if you're an alumni relations person from Harvard, if you'd like to collect a big donation from Lai Yang, if you're the parking attendant in the GXU garage, if you're the gym owner who sells bulk membership to the GXU employees, if you're the pizza delivery guy who delivers $150 truffle pizzas for the GXU Thursday lunch meetings—if you're anyone, anyone, anyone, who profits from GXU's success story continuing, you shut your trap. You smile. You live the lie.

Me: Because you're profiting from the lie…

Keenan: Of course.

Me: But so far, Lai Yang has booked a fake trade. I don't see how a fake trade leads to the entire company being a corrupt entity.

Keenan: GXU Capital.

Me: GXU Capital is the hedge fund connected to GXU?

Keenan: Bingo.

Me: Hang on. I need the bathroom.

-

When I return to the table, Frank Keenan is staring at a blond couple in a booth next to us in the restaurant. They are sucking each other's tongues. The woman has her hands in the man's pants. They are having everything short of sex with their clothes on. Keenan seems unabashed by his interest in this display. He seems totally comfortable with me watching him watch this couple copulate in public.

Me: Tell me about GXU Capital. Why is it the root of all evil?

Keenan: Everything illegal is stuffed in that entity.

Me: Be more precise.

Keenan: GXU Capital started as our "asset management arm." Then it turned into our "hedge fund arm." Then Lai Yang sensed that investors were happier if it was called our "asset management arm," so he went back to calling it that. Asset management sounds official and stable. But what GXU Capital really is is a hedge fund. Or slush fund. Hedge fund. Slush fund. Let's use those terms interchangeably.

Me: Fine. Go on.

Keenan: So GXU Capital is a place. It's where we trade anything and everything we want to trade, in any size, any risk or liquidity profile we desire. There are no rules. We trade with any counterparty, legal or illegal, anywhere in the world. We don't disclose what we do or why we do it, except to brag about it. Profit and loss blur together in a fever dance. GXU Capital is the hedge fund everyone dreams of owning. It's a dream inside a bigger dream.

Me: But you said your auditors comb everything.

Keenan: Yes. Sure. But hedge fund accounting is notoriously complex, and we made complexity a sport. If I showed you the income statement, balance sheet and cash flow statement for one quarter of trading activity at GXU Capital, I doubt you could read it. You couldn't make heads or tails of it.

Me: Lai Yang runs GXU Capital himself?

Keenan: Oh no. Oh no. No, no, no, no, no. Justin Metz runs GXU Capital.

Me: Who is Justin Metz?

Keenan: He's the partner in crime. If Lai Yang is Bonnie, Justin Metz is Clyde. Bonnie and Clyde. If Lai Yang is Butch Cassidy, Justin Metz is the Sundance Kid. Butch Cassidy and the Sundance Kid. Frank and Jesse James. Julius and Ethel Rosenberg. The Lonely Heart Killers. William Burke and William Hare. The Menendez brothers. Leopold and Loeb…

Me: I got it. I understand.

Keenan: And what a partner he is…

Me: Can you be specific?

Keenan: Justin Metz is a wunderkind. Before he arrived at GXU he made so much money trading Treasury derivatives for the bank he worked for—I won't say which bank but everyone knows it—that when he arrived on the trading floor every morning, they chanted "Christ has Risen." At one holiday party for this bank, he wore leather sandals, a brown robe, and carried a staff. Posing as Jesus Christ, he did keg stands while his colleagues whooped and whistled. Citadel, a big client of the bank, tried to hire Justin Metz away *despite the fact* he'd been investigated by the authorities. One year he traded this product, an ETF linked to a bond volatility index. The ETF was exhibiting jagged price moves around Treasury auctions, and everyone knew Justin Metz was talking to someone at the U.S. Treasury and trading on inside information. You know, jamming the ETF price ahead of auction announcements.

Me: Was he charged with anything?

Keenan: No. I just told you. He was paid like $19 million in bonus that year. He made Partner at twenty-six years old. That's a record at that bank.

Me: So, how much did Lai Yang pay to hire him away from this bank?

Keenan: God only knows.

Me: So back to our timeline. 2020, GXU is having real problems. Justin Metz is hired to run GXU Capital. What happens next?

Keenan: A series of very, very bad things.

Me: Name one.

Keenan: Let's start with this. Justin Metz is this big, very good-looking Catholic guy, six foot six, with chestnut hair, from Concord, Massachusetts. Square face. Green eyes. Keyboard player *and* athlete. Power forward for Duke, took a run at the National Title. He was a cheater but whatever. When you look at the guy, you see success. You smell success. When that kind of success is wrapped in success, people just don't ask questions. They want to be in the same room as him. They just want to look at him and understand how he got so many gifts from God. And his parents are good-looking and successful. His siblings are good-looking and smart. He keeps family photos on the Lucite shelves in his office, and people walk in and stare at these people, his family, the whole picture, and think, *How is it possible these people are so perfect and blessed?* So, anyway, what was I saying? Oh yeah. Justin Metz takes over GXU Capital in 2020, the world bends out of shape—I mean, there's a major, major decline in every bourse in March, April, May of that year—and what happens? Justin posts *disgustingly large* trading gains.

Me: He was short the market?

Keenan: Yes. No. Sure. I mean, who cares. We were a Bitcoin trading exchange. We had plans to take the company public. To go public, we needed to prove to the world at large that our *core business* worked. We needed to prove we were making money from our *core business* of matching buyers and sellers of Bitcoin on an exchange, for a fee. We needed to show healthy trading volumes. Healthy fees. Do you know what our core business did during those dog days of 2020? Nothing. Zilch. Zippo. Zero. No one trades Bitcoin when the market is spiraling downward. Bitcoin is a bull market asset. It's a risk-on product. It's a ra-ra-ra-ra-ra party asset. It's not a crisis hedge. Or an inflation hedge. It's not a gold, guns, butter asset that you buy and stash when the world is ending. When the end is upon us, no one will trade Bitcoin.

Me: Are you sure?

Keenan: I have data. We made *zero* from our core business. But we had this other thing. His name was Justin Metz. Justin Metz was doing things his way. He was minting profits…

Me: He was short the stock market?

Keenan: You already asked that.

Me: Well, I'm trying to understand how Metz made so much money for GXU during a period in financial markets when no one made money.

Keenan: Pornography.

Me: Huh?

Keenan: Sure, Metz made *some* money shorting stocks and buying volatility spreads, doing yield curve and coin arbitrage, yadda, yadda, yadda, but *mainly* he made the money in pornography. And online betting.

Me: Sorry, come again…

Keenan: Justin Metz. Pornography. Online betting. The wunderkind had an idea in his head that any corner of the internet that's illegal is probably, most likely, underbanked. He asked the biggest porn vendor in Asia: How much interest do you earn on your deposits? How do you hedge your receivables? How do you buy and sell and hedge your currency exposure? Have you considered your interest rate risk? Then he offered to act as their bank. He provided all these synthetic products, which mimic the offerings from a bank. The products were good. The dollar volumes of transactions in the pornography and betting world are huge. Metz took twenty-five-percent fees and spreads. The opportunity was big and growing. PayPal or Venmo won't touch those businesses. Visa and American Express won't do business with them. So, Justin Metz waded into this big blue ocean of opportunity.

Me: Really? Porn?

Keenan: And online college football betting.

Me: Are you sure?

Keenan: He became a one-man bank. It started as a side-pocket activity, then he liked it so much, he did more of it. It wasn't difficult for him. The guy has a map of the global banking system in his head. It's like asking a plumber how the sink works. It's just pipes. And water. Metz can draw the discount window and Fed Funds and interbank loan market on a napkin, and he can do it for every country in the world. In his sleep, he can convert a one-year mid-curve option on a three-month EURIBOR future to a 2y2y Japanese yen cross-currency swap. He can get non-deliverable yuan trapped in a restricted trade zone in Southern China to a money-market fund in Minneapolis without the Bank of China the wiser. Metz can do anything.

Me: Sorry. I want to backtrack a second.

Keenan: Backtrack away.

Me: You're telling me GXU is in the pornography business?

Keenan: I'm telling you GXU *banks* the pornography business.

Me: And Lai Yang gave this his blessing?

Keenan: Not really. No. Well. Yes. But it didn't happen right away. Metz made all this money, but he didn't *fully disclose* to Lai Yang how he made the money.

Me: So, okay. When did he tell Lai Yang what he was up to?

Keenan: Q3 2020. Lai Yang knew Justin Metz was up to something. He looked at the daily P&L sheets. Then Lai Yang had a fit. He threw a tantrum in the conference room. Because he understood nothing. Or he understood that he didn't understand what Justin Metz was doing. We were all there that day. Ask any employee who was working on the floor at GXU that afternoon in Palo Alto if they remember when Lai Yang had a conniption. He absolutely hit the ceiling. Lost his composure. He threw his fist into the glass and because it was triple-reinforced glass—it was totally soundproof—he broke fingers. He screwed up his hand. It must have hurt because his face turned ghost-white. Rage isn't the word. It was worse than that. Justin Metz flew out of the building and Lai Yang chased him. Car chase. Fight.

Me: You have evidence of this?

Keenan: Someone sent us a TikTok video. They were both in sports cars. Lai Yang ran down Justin Metz on the road. Vehicle collision. They got out and started pounding each other on one of the public lawn spaces in Palo Alto.

Me: Do you still have the video?

Keenan: You can find it online. You can also check the Palo Alto police records. Anyway, when they realized the public nature of what they were doing, they retreated. They went to Metz's home. That night, they made up. They must have resolved their differences.

Me: How do you know this?

Keenan: Listen, lady. The fact pattern is this: The two founders get into a huge, rip-roaring fight. The next day, GXU was a different company. Hundred-percent different company.

Me: I need more than that.

Keenan: Let's get dessert first.

Our waitress was back. Now she had sweat globules on her lip. Frank asks politely about dessert. She looks sad and confused. She tells him they only have Baked Alaska for four people. Frank asks if the chef can halve it? Twenty minutes later—we'd given up, we'd left cash on the table and were leaving—she emerges wearing burned oven mitts clutching a thirty-pound dish of flaming ice cream. The flames leap into her face. The dessert comes crashing down. Two spoons are thrown in our direction. To that point, my meal had been inedible, so I wasn't going to venture into dessert. Frank felt differently. He dug his spoon down into the concoction. He lifted a heap of alcohol-covered ice cream.

Frank: This is excellent. You're not going to try it?

-

At 2 a.m. we take a break and go to the casino. We'd consumed so much caffeine that neither of us could sleep. We chose Pai Gow poker, a slow game played with a fifty-two-card deck and a single joker. The dealer, a white skinny guy with cold sores and blond, cotton-candy-floss hair, talked too much between games. It was unorthodox how much he talked while fingering the cards. He made weird overtures. He told us that in some places Pai Gow poker is played with dominoes, and if we wanted to play with dominoes, we could go back to his place later. I ordered whiskey to take the edge off. Frank drank gin.

Me: So, by 2021 at GXU, there was gross accounting fraud, major profits coming from pornography that your accountants and lawyers claim were coming from somewhere else—but in your defense, you sent a letter to the SEC?

Keenan: I did.

Me: I'm imagining your defense.

Keenan: Off the record, I'll tell you, I knew a lot more than I put in that letter. But it didn't matter. The SEC didn't care…

Me: Where did you get that idea?

Keenan: I tried to alert the SEC in 2019. They didn't care. I tried again in 2020 and got no response. Then I made so much money that I stopped caring. You need to understand something. I was fifty years old. I was happy. I had millions in the bank and my stock options were worth the moon. My reputation as an economist, a philosopher, a thinker, an author of ideas—well, my reputation was soaring. I hired an assistant to keep track of how popular I was. The invitations to parties and podcasts and conferences kept rolling in. Invitations, invitations, more invitations. It was like nothing I'd ever experienced. One day I was a dusty, obscure, loser weirdo economist working in a dark lecture hall at the University of Chicago. No one respects economists. Let's be honest. Next thing I know, I'm a celebrity. I got invited to an Oscars afterparty. I got an invitation to the Met Gala. Who would believe it?

Me: Were you living a big lifestyle?

Keenan: Yes! Of course! I had so many new friends! People wanted to hang out! Interesting, successful people who spent a lot of money and had interesting, big lives. I was flying here and there and everywhere. Everyone asked me *what I thought about everything!!!* I mean, I can't tell you how happy I was. My body felt bionic.

Me: Was everyone at GXU flying high?

Keenan: We'd come through the pandemic like heroes. The original employees of GXU were *buying jets*. I mean, it was considered normal *to buy a jet*. Lai Yang was a deity. His confidence was growing. He told everyone that within five years the U.S. Dollar would cease to exist and there would be only Bitcoin, and when there was only Bitcoin, there was only us. GXU. We hit peak valuation. The hype around GXU was parabolic.

Me: Yes, the world loved him.

Keenan: The world *still* loves Lai Yang. Despite what you and I are talking about here, even if this comes out, there will be a period of disbelief. Lai Yang has carved out his place in the American mind; he's the man taking us into the future.

Me: Sure, but when I send a forensic accountant your way....

Keenan: No. GXU is at the "frontier of human possibility." Investors are rich and fat and happy. My colleagues *believe* that in a few short years, they've *truly, honestly, really, in earnest* built the next great innovation in financial markets. They built the first Bitcoin exchange! If the Dutch settlers could see them now! The old, stale Wall Street will bend the knee! Because GXU can do everything better.

Me: I have a stomachache.

Keenan: You want another drink?

-

We were back in Frank's hotel suite. He was drunk, very damaged, and I still didn't have my own room. The pull-out couch was my only option. I stood at the atlas on the wall, plucking neon-colored threads. Keenan knocked around the room in search of something.

Me: I need to tell you something.

Keenan: What?

Me: This evidence you've collected. It isn't enough.

Keenan: What do you want from me?

Me: I'm going to show this report to the Commission, but if I'm honest with you, I think they're going to ask for more. They'll want you to go back to work at GXU. They'll want you to feed us live information until we have enough to act. They'll want you to wear a wire.

Keenan: Good luck.

Me: What you mean good luck?

Keenan: Good luck getting me to wear a wire. Do you have any idea what kind of person Lai Yang has turned into? He has gangster bodyguards protecting him now. If he catches me wearing a wire, he'll rip my guts out through my nose. Honestly, I'd rather spend a year in white-collar prison. Reading the Bible and the complete works of Shakespeare.

Me: That might happen. If you don't agree to our terms.

We stood facing each other. Frank was drooling drunk, and he'd found the thing he was searching for. A serene look crossed his face. Pleasure. Calm. Like he'd passed gas. Or he'd had an orgasm. He shook several pills from orange bottle onto his palm.

Keenan: You want to do Adderall? We can watch the sun rise....

-

I woke up with a blinding hangover. White sun burned a hole through the slat blinds. A snowplow was scraping the parking lot; the sound of metal on asphalt exploded my ears. When I peered out the window, I saw the vehicle was making mountains of hard-packed snow, salt, ice, and rock and forming giant walls that trapped cars in their parking spaces.

I jumped to my feet. I didn't want my rental car trapped. I needed to get out of here. I needed to escape this cut-rate casino and get to my laptop so I could type up this report. Then I needed to fly to Washington, D.C., to present to the Commission. Dry heat blasted down from the ceiling vent. My head felt like boiled cabbage. The metal coils of the pull-out couch had rendered my spine immobile. Frank emerged through his bedroom door. His teeth chattered. His beard glistened with sweat. I couldn't tell if he'd slept.

Keenan: You're leaving me?

Me: I need to go to work. Washington, D.C.

Keenan: So, what's next?

Me: Do you remember what I asked you to do last night?

Keenan: I don't want to go back to work for GXU. I'll get killed there.

Me: We'll protect you.

Frank Keenan grew embarrassed. His neck bloomed pink. He shuffled his feet.

Me: I'm sorry this happened to you. You seem like a good person.

Keenan: As Chairman Mao said, too soon to tell.

I nodded solemnly. I left the room. I rolled my weekend bag onto the elevator, which smelled of Windex. Someone had vomited where I was standing. There were still hot pink chunks stuck to the rug near my feet. I pressed the button marked "Lobby" with my elbow.

Back in the entrance of the hotel I stood near a row of fake palm trees and watched a light blizzard blow in through the electric doors. The glass doors opened and shut according to their own plan. No one was coming or going. The slot machines were ringing emptily behind me. I was about to check out when I remembered I didn't need to check out. There was no bill to pay. As I passed the front desk, a man in a stiff red uniform burst forward. He was the proud manager of Executive Stay & Play Suites. He held forth a gargantuan set of keys.

"Hey! You! I called you twice! I have a room available. The Rose Suite just opened and it has your name on it!" he declared victoriously.

"Not a chance," I said and left.

Chapter Three. Diary of a Prosecutor on the Run

In October, I lost the biggest case of my career. Why the jury did not believe the man was guilty I was not told. So it went; I lost the case, my reputation, and my personal safety. I couldn't ride the subway or sit at a restaurant without his assailants circling me. After months of being stalked sunup to sundown, I lost my ability to concentrate. I was unable to take new cases. Eventually, the dysfunction bled into my bank account and marriage. Until that moment, I hadn't realized the two were linked—but if I couldn't work and be myself, my husband didn't want me around, and if he didn't want me around, then I needed a custody lawyer because we had an eight-year-old daughter I wasn't going to leave behind.

The custody lawyer was a friend from school, and after I described how narrowly I'd avoided losing my legs to a black limo traveling sixty miles per hour toward me on Third Avenue, she advised me to put personal safety first.

That's how I ended up on this island in Maine.

I moved here with a new phone number, laptop, and a duffel bag of clothing. I brought the dog. I tell myself each day the situation is temporary, and it occurs to me this is as permanent a temporary situation as I've ever endured. If I want to get off the island I have to call Bob Trawley's water taxi that runs four times a day in the summer, once a day in the fall, and never from November to May. If Bob comes to get me, it's because I've called five times and promised to pay three times his normal rate, and even then he shows up a day late and in a bad mood. He's awoken from a deep alcoholic slumber, a time-honored technique of getting through the winter here, and he's not happy to see me. His hands are covered in engine grease.

Still, I'm able to get my groceries.

Then I go home, cook spaghetti for me and the dog, and think about all the ways I could have avoided this fate.

-

I've been writing essays to pass the time. The essays aren't good but they are current. An interior designer I once met on the subway told me there are three virtues—fast, good, and cheap. Of the three, you can pick two but not all three. If you want a good desk at a cheap price, it'll take a year to find. If you want a good desk tomorrow, you can have it, but you'll pay an exorbitant price. This is how I'm thinking about my essays.

-

Angel Woodrow is the man I tried to put in prison. He's the reason I'm on this island. The U.S. Attorney's Office for the Southern District charged him with one count of sex trafficking of a minor and one count of conspiracy to commit sex trafficking. You may have read about it in *United States of America v. Angel Woodrow*. If you did, I won't bore you with details you know. I'll limit myself to facts too strange for the jury to consider.

Here's one fact: Angel didn't look like a sex trafficker. He was an effete man: five feet and a hundred pounds with baby powder skin and manicured nails. He wore doll clothes: tiny suits and polished shoes, and one of his friends told me he was the best-dressed man in church. Some days he wore cerulean cufflinks, other days, a silk tie and a gold pen slipped in his pocket, or a pair of suspenders with gold lamé. Never did he wear these in combination, however, because Angel had a sixth sense for how to manage impressions. He sat upright and spoke in a low, careful whisper. He kept his eye contact humble and true. When I asked him about his upbringing, he said his father had a lot of money, but he was taught as a kid the worst thing is life is to be boastful. When he answered questions, he possessed calm. The more difficult the question, the calmer he was. Angel never interrupted. He never changed his breathing. He never gave a sign he had to *think*; no verbal tic, no eyelid flutter, no touching of the face or craning of the neck or angling of the torso. In all the hours I faced him, I'm ashamed to say, every word—absolutely every word that escaped his mouth—sounded like the truth.

This presented a problem for me.

Because another fact about Angel Woodrow is that he was an upstanding member of society. He's an excellent businessman. Angel inherited from his father a network of nursing homes: Golden Care Inc., Golden Care Plus, and Dawn Life. The business—which offered a range of services, assisted living for healthy sixty-year-olds to palliative care and hospice care for the nearly dead—was broken when Angel inherited it. The facilities were crumbling. The board was in open revolt. Lawsuit after lawsuit after lawsuit poured in from patients and families of patients who had been ripped off, mistreated, abused, or left for dead. Angel told CNBC nine hundred and ninety-nine people out of a thousand, given the exact circumstances, would have given up. They would have let the business die.

But Angel didn't. He fired his board. He whittled his workforce down to fifty employees. He razed the facilities he couldn't afford, which were all of them, except two. Two facilities were receiving favorable tax treatment: an assisted-living home in Niagara Falls, New York, and a hospice center in Fort Lee, New Jersey. Angel kept these open. He made tiny adjustments day after day, knowing a solution would come to him. Then one day he did the big thing.

In Fort Lee, Angel set up a call center. With the free help of dying patients who lived there and had nothing to do all day, he conducted a guerilla cold-call survey of 100,000 senior citizens across America about conditions in their facilities. His questionnaire was designed by a psychiatrist named Simon Welch, and the "Welch questionnaire," as it came to be known, was so acute, so incisive in its rooting out of information—that it won Angel fame. He packaged and sold the information to the largest healthcare conglomerates in the world and used proceeds to borrow and rebuild his own facilities. Within five years he had the biggest network of nursing homes in New York, New Jersey, and Pennsylvania.

"Angel's Miracle" was the name of the Wharton Business School case study that detailed Angel's turnaround of a dead business. The IPO made him rich. It landed him many a politician friend. It also landed him on the cover of *Crain's New York Business* in April of 2015.

-

Helen Hidalgo, an underage employee of Golden Care, Inc., boarded the PATH train at Newark-Penn Station one day and sat next to me. She had the issue of *Crain's New York Business* folded under her arm. She didn't talk to me. She just sat there, all the way from Newark-Penn Station to Journal Square to Exchange Place in lower Manhattan. The next day, I was working the same schedule from the same office in Newark, and she found me. She sat next to me. Same woman same newspaper. Then the weekend came. I didn't see her.

There's a rule on the New York City Subway: You can look at someone for as long as you like but as soon as the person makes eye contact you can never look at them again. I was careful never to look at Helen Hidalgo. I knew she wanted my help with something. I knew she hadn't yet worked up the courage to ask me for help.

That weekend must have been a bad one for Helen. Because Monday afternoon when she boarded the PATH train, she put the newspaper in my lap. There was Angel Woodrow, staring up at me, smiling.

-

It's twenty-eight degrees today on the island. The sky is thunderous black. The beach is ice. My dog is so depressed he won't go for a walk so I'm sitting here, reading through my early case notes on Angel Woodrow. It's amazing to me now, as I review facts on his religious upbringing, the car he drives, how he met each woman and what he said to them—that when I took these notes I didn't know I'd lose the case. I see on the pages of this notebook, in my word choice and hand scrawl, that I was optimistic. I bet if you opened the notebook of anyone who has embarked on a great project and failed—you'll see a graveyard of optimism like the one I'm staring at now. One whole page is devoted to the question: "Did Helen know Wanda?" and the way I double-underlined the question mark shows me what I thought. I thought the question opened a universe and in that universe I'd find everything.

How wrong I was.

On another page I wrote, "Read E. Bern's book." I remember going to Strand bookstore to find that book, and my sharp disappointment as I stood in the basement, scanning the text, that of 140 pages only eight were devoted to sex games. In the chapter on sex games, not a word—not a single word—illuminated the mind of Angel Woodrow.

All great lawyers talk about process. How superior process leads to superior results. But no one talks about Fate. I've read every note in this notebook, and nowhere, nowhere, have I found the note that says: *Watch out.*

-

Helen Hidalgo was born in Balabac Palawan, a mountainous, malaria-ridden island in the Philippines. She was sixteen when she came to this country with a backpack, a GSM phone, and thirty dollars in a Ziplock bag. She has burnt-brown skin, wide-set green eyes, and an easy laugh. She's almost six feet, which is unheard of for a Filipina. She said in her village her nickname was "The Olympic swimmer," and she laughs when she says it because she can't, in fact, swim. She was never taught. Helen had school until eighth grade but she wasn't a student; she didn't have a head for numbers and couldn't sit still to read. She came to the U.S. because her sister was here. The sister told Helen there were jobs available.

If geography is destiny then Helen's worked in reverse.

Newark, New Jersey, is one of the poorest cities in the nation. Helen spent her first three years in a zip code that on a per-capita basis registers below Balabac Palawan, the island she came from. It was a different kind of poor—Helen described to me—in her village there was hardship but no one felt ashamed of their life. Exactly the opposite was true in Newark; what Helen saw around her frightened her. The city was filthy and dangerous and disorganized, and no one cared what happened to anyone else.

Helen was lucky, in this sense, to find the dormitory she lived in for three years. It was run by a Filipina woman for Filipina women. She lived in a dorm room with bunk beds and depending on who had days off from live-in domestic jobs, the rooms held any-where from two to twenty women. Some nights were peaceful. Other nights were hell. But Helen knew the language and the smells of the women around her, and on days off, she had company. There was a courtyard with a poplar tree, and in it they sat playing Pusoy (a card game), shopping for flash clearance clothes on an iPad, cooking chicken rice porridge, and calling family on free video chat. There was a rhythm to life.

One day, at the end of her shift at the hospice center, Helen was on her way to the bus stop when a man approached her. He said his name was Angel Woodrow and he owned this hospice center and many others. Helen didn't believe him because the man was smaller than a minute, but then her boss walked up. The boss tried to impress Angel. Helen paid attention. Then Angel asked Helen how she liked her job. He invited her into his black Chevy Tahoe. He said he was going to get drinks with friends and he offered her a ride home. When she got in the car, she felt comfortable. Angel was calm about it.

They drove around in his Tahoe for an hour. They bought food at an Arby's drive-thru forty minutes from where she worked. They met up with two of Angel's friends, who she never saw again, at a

Hooters-type bar. They had drinks. Helen remembers she ordered a pink non-alcoholic drink, but as she sipped it, she felt her cheeks flush. It was late, maybe midnight, when they drove to one of Angel's houses—he explained he had many houses, but he didn't explain why he was taking her to one in Rockland County, New York. When they got there, she saw the big white gates and the three-story Disneyland structure. Then he showed her the house. Dozens of rooms with gold furniture and grand pianos. They stood in the kitchen for a while. Angel asked Helen if she'd like to see his basement. She said yes not knowing the English word for "basement."

When they got down to the basement, Helen thought it looked like a child's playroom. There was a red circle carpet, an easel with days of the week on quilt squares, a toy bin, a big wardrobe with dress-up clothes and a wooden stage. The stage had lights and painted steps you could step onto, to pretend you were on a mountain range or on a ship out to sea. There were play chairs facing the stage, and on one chair was a stuffed turtle. The turtle was propped unnaturally on its back, to watch the stage.

Angel asked without embarrassment if Helen wanted to play a game. She didn't want to disappoint him, so she said yes. He chose a cowboy outfit for himself. He selected a blue gingham dress with corset, garter belt and stockings for her. He gave her a script to read. Helen's English was bad, but she tried her best. The script went like this:

Cowboy: Come and see the barn.

Western Woman: I've loved barns ever since I was a little girl.

For an hour, they practiced these lines. Angel didn't like the way she sounded. He kept repeating her lines for her. Sometimes he impersonated Western Woman's accent or showed her how to touch her breasts and flirt. He was never violent. He said it was critical

Helen understand that *she controlled the interaction*. She didn't know what this meant and wouldn't for years, until an NYU psychiatrist friend of mine told us why this this game works.

Around 2 a.m. Helen asked to go home. Angel went to get his keys upstairs and said he'd be back. Helen heard the basement door lock. Five minutes later, she heard a car engine. She remembers looking through the barred window in the basement to see his taillights leave the driveway. She realized, too late, that her phone and bag were upstairs.

Her first thought, Helen said, was that he'd made a mistake. It was late. Angel might have been drunk or forgotten she was there. He would realize his mistake and come back. Later, Helen's mind drifted to the TV shows she'd seen. The news clips about women locked in predators' basements. She panicked and cried until she fell asleep. She doesn't know how long she was out for, but when she woke up, the sun was high in the sky, she could hear water rushing through pipes in the drywall, crickets somewhere—in the basement or just outside—and she knew Angel wasn't coming back. She looked for a way out. She punched the door, ripped the insulation in the stairwell, and threw a chair against a window. When she'd exhausted herself, she cried dry tears. She scavenged for food. Finally, she lay, despondent, on the red circle carpet.

When she woke, Angel stood over her. He paid her and let her go.

-

No one should be in this part of Maine in April. My husband said it before I left, and I've been at my desk wondering if he'll ever call. Two people in the world know how to get in touch with me: my boss, who announced he's running for state attorney and won't call, and my husband, who I think won't call.

Our marriage is a tangle of thorns.

If you can believe it, the NYU psychiatrist friend of mine, the one who elucidated, *Each individual has available three ego states which are not roles but psychological realities—Parent, Adult, and Child, and at any given moment an individual can shift ego states between P, A, or C*—this friend was having an affair with my husband.

Or I should say, my husband was having an affair with her.

When I brought the Angel Woodrow puzzle to her, she did not tell me she was sleeping with my husband. What she said was: *The most gratifying forms of social contact are games and intimacy. Intimacy is difficult to achieve. Even a mother cannot hold eye contact with her infant for more than ten seconds. So people play games. Family and marriage and work life, year after year, are based on games. Play may be grimly serious, or even fatally serious—*

The page after that is ripped out. I must have been angry at her.

-

Angel Woodrow paid Helen $2,900 for staying locked in his basement for two nights. He paid her in cash, a mix of hundreds and fifties, and the sum changed her life. Immediately, she moved into an apartment in Jersey City with her sister and a roommate who had a good job. Helen had her own room and half bathroom. She went upstairs to shower but she had the shower to herself for as long as she wanted. She could keep her bath sponge and body wash there and no one touched it. She bought fruit for the refrigerator and a blender to make smoothies. She paid for yoga class. She bought new sheets. She got promoted at work and was suddenly getting better shifts and a ten percent larger paycheck.

For the first time, she felt *American* in the sense people talked about.

While Helen was cooking noodles one night, she started to cry. She heard footsteps outside her apartment. She knew it wasn't her roommate or sister because they had left for work. She heard him outside the door. His voice was calm. "—I'm not going to hurt you. I just want to say I'm sorry." Helen slipped a kitchen knife in her back pocket and stood at the door. He kept repeating it. "—I just want to say I'm sorry." Helen kept the chain on the door.

"It's fine," she said quietly, hoping he'd go away. But Angel didn't go away. He begged to come inside. He said if she let him in, he'd give her a gift.

No sooner did she unhook the chain than a 300-pound man with a ponytail and tattoos crashed through the door and bludgeoned her on the head. Helen hit the floor. She remembers being dragged to the service elevator. She remembers crying out. She remembers hearing Angel's voice as a vinegar-soaked rag was stuffed in her mouth.

-

That night, the game was called Father and Teenage Daughter. Angel wore a plaid sports jacket, skinny tie, and chunky glasses, and Helen wore a poodle skirt, bobby socks, and saddle shoes. She also wore handcuffs because she'd tried to scratch Angel's face off. While Helen choked and cried, Angel explained the game. The Father is irate. Teenage Girl came home too late and refuses to be interrogated. The script is:

Father: Where the hell have you been?
Teenage Daughter: With Sally.
Father: That wasn't Sally's car that dropped you off.
Teenage Daughter: It was Sally's friend.
Father: I've never seen that car.
Teenage Daughter: Because you don't know Sally's friend.

If Helen forgot her lines or refused to play her part, Angel went upstairs and came back with the ponytailed man. The ponytailed man beat Helen into submission. This went on until, through bloody teeth and split tongue, Helen learned her lines. She played the part of Teenage Daughter and she played it well. Angel seemed satisfied.

-

Hail. This island is being attacked so I can't go outside. I'm stuck at my desk.

For that reason, I embarked on a new project. I found a printer in the closet, a rickety one that jams every twenty pages, and I've printed out files from every case I've ever lost. Angel Woodrow wasn't enough for me. I had to go back further.

It's amazing what you find.

In 2016, I prosecuted a man who killed his wife for *vagina dentata*; on the stand, he told everyone that her vagina had teeth. Every time they "fornicated" he considered self-defense, until one day he had no choice but to kill her. The jury listened with interest. The defense lawyer, a Canadian in a tweed suit with arm patches, a baritone voice, and Lucite eyeglasses, made the point: There was no weapon and no motive. Which is strange, because the weapon was there in an evidence bag and it had been matched, fingerprint and DNA, to the man on the stand. Stranger still was why he didn't pursue an NGRI strategy: not guilty by reason of insanity. That, in my opinion, would have been reasonable. The Canadian instead treated his client with sobriety and respect, and as the trial progressed, the judge and jury did the same.

After the whole thing finished, I asked the lawyer how he did it. How he created a new universe with new rules, and he gave me a straight look and said, "You had your chance."

-

I asked my NYU psychiatrist friend to be an expert witness on the case. The mind of Angel Woodrow was like a math problem she'd solved twenty years ago. The Cowboy game, for instance—

Cowboy: Come and see the barn.

Western Woman: I've loved barns ever since I was a little girl.

She showed two diagrams to the courtroom. First, a diagram illustrating a "transaction": ADULT and ADULT with an arrow between. Then: ADULT and CHILD with an arrow between. She explained that at the social level it's a conversation about barns, but at the psychological level it's a Child conversation about sex play. On the surface the Adult has the initiative, but as in most games, the outcome is determined by the Child, and the participants may be in for a surprise.

Father and Teenage Daughter was simple. If Father and Teenage Daughter live in the same house, they must find reasons to pick arguments and slam doors—or else they'll be forced to recognize their sexual love. They play a game called "violent fight" to avoid recognizing their attraction.

-

I'm reading *Eichmann in Jerusalem* now, because the hail won't stop and the only thing that calms my nerves is war or plague or genocide literature. The story is: Adolf Eichmann, a Nazi with rotten teeth and a receding hairline, goes to Jerusalem, where he stands trial for scheduling the trains that sent six million Jews to their deaths. He gets bored in prison. He asks the guards for something to read. They give him Nabokov's *Lolita*, which was just then an international sensation. Eichmann reads fifty pages of the masterwork and hands the book back to the prison guard. The guard looks dismayed. You didn't like it?

Eichmann answers in German: *Das ist aber ein sehr unerfreuliches buch.*

In English: "It is quite an unwholesome book."

-

For six months, Helen lived in a trance. She combed her hair. She went to work. She came home and ate cereal in front of the TV. When she slept, she slept in two-hour blocks of nightmares and woke up soaked in sweat. Then she'd shower, smoke cigarettes at the window, and watch the road to see if Angel's men were coming for her. Some nights she did this until the sun came up. Other nights she drank a bottle of NyQuil and passed out.

It was all Helen could do to keep her sister out of it. Angel said he would pay Helen to recruit her sister. When Helen resisted— when she tried to scratch his throat or ears—Angel liked it. If Helen spat on his face, Angel took a spool of fishing line and banded her wrists so tightly, she lost circulation. Right when she thought she'd lose her hands, he whispered, "If you ever call the police, your sister will die."

Helen knew there were other victims; she'd found a long blond hair strung in the carpet of one basement she slept in. She found a pile of nail clippings, with bits of red nail polish on the end. Helen didn't know if the victims were women—she assumed they were—and she didn't know if they were alive or dead. She didn't want to know.

It was with hesitation that Helen took notice of a coworker, a young Haitian named Wanda, who was acting out and making egregious mistakes at work. She broke a bed. She broke a window when she was moving a respirator. She moved a patient into an easy chair and left the room, not noticing his foot was smothered between the chair and the wall. When the next shift discovered the mistake, the foot nearly had to be amputated.

When Wanda was confronted by her boss, she broke into violent crying jags. Her wailing could be heard throughout the halls. The nurses gossiped about it. Why wasn't Wanda being fired? Helen ignored the gossip; she didn't want to know more.

Helen was at the bus stop one night when she saw Wanda at the edge of the parking lot with two girls who looked like teenagers. While Helen was watching, the bus arrived. Helen decided to stay to see what happened. Three buses came and went. Helen stood, watching Wanda and the two girls wait. Just as Helen was about to give up and go home, she saw it. The black Chevy Tahoe pulled up next to Wanda.

For a week, Helen lived with the agony of indecision. She wanted to approach Wanda. She wanted to talk to someone—anyone—about the nightmare that plagued her existence; but every time she sought Wanda out at work, she decided the woman was crazy. Batshit crazy. Her eyes were bloodshot. She was always breaking things and yelling. Helen saw Wanda beat a man who was almost dead. Helen was afraid of her.

Helen didn't do anything.

In December that year, as plastic menorahs and Christmas trees were taken from boxes and installed in the common area—as Helen was stringing lights around a window—she heard the nurses talking. Wanda was found dead in her car at 5 a.m. She'd drunk a quart of bleach.

-

Twice yesterday, I saw a black boat in the distance, motoring toward me. I called the Coast Guard and explained the situation. They told me to call the police. I called the police who told me to call the Coast Guard.

I have a friend in Deer Isle, Maine, who used to run the CIA. Very few people know this but Deer Isle, Maine, is where the 1950s, '60s, and '70s intelligence community now lives. Many are dead from old age but the ones who are alive are perfectly safe. The reason is they specialize in survival. They've studied their worst enemy (in some cases, it's a politician in the U.S. government) and they've set up systems of bribes and threats. It's an art more than a science, and no zip code in the world has more geriatrics who specialize in the art of bribe-and-threat survival. Tomorrow, my friend from Deer Isle will arrive. His boat is blue, so I'll know the difference.

-

Wanda's suicide helped Helen. It helped her go to the police. She went to the Third Precinct in Newark and insisted on seeing a female officer. The cops gave her a hard time about this; they weren't in the habit of changing protocol for a Filipina with no cash in her pocket. But Helen was desperate. And insistent. She'd speak to a woman officer only. The cops told her she could wait as long as she wanted in the catching area; she could sleep there, for all they cared. She came back the next day and the next day and the next day. Finally, a female officer took her in a concrete room with no windows.

Helen laid out her story carefully. She told the officer everything she knew about Angel Woodrow; how he'd approached her. Where he'd taken her. What he had done to her. How much she was paid. Then she described his conspirators. She gave specific detail, enough that any "employee" of Angel's could be identified in a lineup. She gave the license plate of the black Chevy Tahoe and said there must be hair and nail and skin samples in the backseat and in the trunk. She told the officer about Wanda St. Jean Pierre, about her suicide, and she brought the name of the morgue where Wanda's body was taken. The officer wrote everything down. She brought two investigators in the room who asked Helen questions. They all left the room. When they came back, they said they'd call Helen the next day.

They never called.

-

I visited the Golden Care, Inc. nursing home in Wilkes-Barre, Pennsylvania, before I had a permit to do so. The entrance was painted canary yellow and a corporate credo hung on the wall: *Make Integrity Your Pledge.* I met the director. I told her I was looking at homes for my aging mother. She gave me a tour and confirmed a fact I already knew: this was the original facility. Angel Woodrow's father, Gene Woodrow, purchased the land after the war. His intent was to make it a psychiatric hospital. During World War Two, Gene had worked in a field ward treating men who lost their minds in combat. He wanted to continue this work after the war. But at the last minute, he changed the permit to "Assisted Care Living." That was a relatively new concept at the time, in that era. Gene was an incredible man and he cared deeply about his community. He bought a house near the facility, married a beautiful Presbyterian woman and started a family.

That night, in room 433 of the Tides Motor Inn in Wilkes-Barre, a detective told me Angel's father was a tyrannical, abusive psychopath. Everyone in town knew it, including the priest at his wife's church. Gene Woodrow kept his privacy by donating every dollar he ever made to politicians, the church, and the Rotary Club. It was rumored he had a torture chamber in his basement and subjected his family to violence.

For not much money, I paid the owner of Angel Woodrow's childhood home to let me see the basement. The owner said he bought the house out of foreclosure. When he moved in, the basement had decades-old plumbing, hydronics and electrical. The Woodrow family had lived there, vacated it, put it in trust, then sold it. By the time he got there, the basement was so filled with junk, he paid a contractor to help him excavate it. I asked if he'd seen anything strange then—or any time since—and he walked me to a crawl space where the contractor had left an old boiler intact. "One thing," he said, pointing behind the boiler.

There, scratched into the wall was a message. It said—
I'm Johnny, the child who lied.

-

When they came for Helen at 2 a.m., she was prepared. She had 9-1-1 on speakerphone. The ponytailed man laughed as she pointed the phone at him. He grabbed her, roped her arms together and put her in the trunk of his car.

She spent the weekend in Angel's basement. The game he wanted to play was hide-and-seek. She was Father and he was Child. If Father found Child too easily, Angel would shout and berate Helen. He said, Father has to be a good player and hold off so Child can give a clue by calling out, dropping something or banging. That way, Child forces Father to find him but shows chagrin and surprise at being found. If the game is not played correctly, he explained, there's no suspense or fun. After hours of hide-and-seek, Helen was bruised, beaten and delirious. She made a mistake. She came around a corner and found Angel too easily, and when she did, he pointed a gun at her head. That Monday, she found me on the E train. She was shaking.

-

The first question I asked Helen on April 27 after we exited the subway, got Greek coffee from a vendor on Lafayette and walked to a bench at the reflective pool in Collect Pond Park was this: "Are there other victims?"

-

File the notice of appeal. That's all that I'm trying to accomplish. I lugged a dozen storage boxes to this island with witness transcripts, police reports, evidence—every court record I could steal and copy. Photos of everyone we deposed. Everyone who offered to testify, and those who didn't. Now I'm staring at the mess, wondering, how do I do this?

-

4 a.m. is the best time to work. I work in a goose-down jacket and ski hat. I have enough coffee and amphetamines to last me a month. If I read my notes on the case material, start to finish, if I review my steps and missteps, I can form a strategy.

This takes training and discipline.

Also, there's the matter of my assailant.

I sleep in running shoes. When I'm not writing, I practice my escape; push-ups, v-ups, pull-ups, sprints, I's, Y's and T's, and extreme temperature shocks. I've strung a duffel to the pine tree left of the mailbox with an eight-inch hunting knife, two passports, and $50,000 in U.S. and Canadian dollars. It's a quarter mile to the mailbox, fifteen feet to the duffel, and fifty feet to a trailhead across the road. That trail runs a mile through the woods to the north side of the island. From there it nosedives off a cliff into the ocean. Left, is a white clapboard church. The church has cell service. If the weather is clear, then I can arrange a pick-up from below that ledge. If the fog is thick or thunder clouds roll in, if the boat can't reach shore—if I get lost, poisoned, drowned, or shot in the back by a sniper—I copied 19,000 documents to an encrypted flash drive and taped it to the electrical panel inside room 12 at the Acadia Mountain Inn. This I'll tell my friend with the blue boat when he arrives.

-

Bryn W. Gillis is my name. It's bled all over the press. I'm five feet nine inches, 117 pounds, and thirty-eight years old. I caught myself in the mirror just now. It's a horror image. I used to be a healthy-looking woman with shiny hair and olive skin. High cheekbones. Clear eyes. My back was straight and my shoulders strong.

Now I'm stooped over. My frame is collapsed inwards. There's a blood vessel popped in my left eyeball, from stress paranoia and exhaustion. Dark shadows swallow my cheeks. My hair is thin and black with grease. A cold sore blooms on my lip. My hands tremble.

-

"Bryn. Are you having dreams about the case?"

"Yes."

I'm on the phone with one of my mentors, my former professor, who followed every twist and turn of the case.

"Are your dreams vivid and powerful?" he asks.

"Yes."

"Write them down. Dreams can be revelations."

At 3 a.m., I wrote down two dreams. The first was about a man ejaculating in a flowerpot outside a restaurant. The cops see him and walk past. In the second dream, I'm back in the courtroom. I'm giving opening arguments to the jury. My husband's lover is in the witness box, nodding at me. I say the following: *Let's look at the example of Johnny, the child who lied.* While his parents and their friends were drinking coffee at the kitchen table, Johnny, age five, ran in and out of the room, happily pulling his favorite truck behind. Suddenly, there was a crash in the living room. Entering that room, his mother found a glass vase knocked off the coffee table and shattered.

"Who did that?" she asked.

"Doggie," he replied.

Mother's neck reddens. She knew she had let the dog out five minutes earlier. Stepping forward, she hit him, saying, "I will not have a child who lies!"

I turn to the defendant's table. Angel Woodrow is smiling at me, and in his lap is my daughter. She has black blood running from her eyes.

I yell and wake up.

Chapter Four. Love Was her Name

It was not a minute past 6 a.m. Both Caro and her boyfriend, Gerry, were due at work within the hour. Their sex, hot and passionate, was prolonged. Gerry rolled his brawny, compact frame over. He stuck his blond duck fuzz hair under the pillow. He slammed the snooze button. Caro, her jade skin naked and sweaty, sat up. Her pointy A-cup boobs stuck out like arrows. Out of breath, she swung her thick legs to the floor. *Ten minutes to shower and get dressed, get a coffee. Wet hair in a ponytail. No makeup today.* Caro decided she'd save time as she lifted a towel from the floor and wrapped it around her waist. She poked a finger through the blinds to look out the window. The sun was coming up over cracked and oily asphalt. The dogwood trees of University Heights were in bloom. The branches erupted in heavy pink blossoms.

"Do I have to drag you into the shower?" she chided Gerry. He was still a lump under the blanket. "Okay, fine, you tell Calabro why you're late again—" Caro said as she slid the door shut to the bathroom.

"Happy to tell him," Gerry called out.

Gerry was in his third year as a crime scene investigator. Caro was in her third year in evidence control. They'd met at College Point. They'd never been romantically interested in each other until a rainy night in March when they worked the same crime scene. A deranged bank teller had opened fire on two customers using an ATM machine in a hip, upscale neighborhood in Jersey City. The man chased the customers out of the bank, onto the street, into a crowd. There he shot at them. Gerry and Caro were called immediately to the scene, where they spent the night inside the yellow police tape, combing flashlights over the pavement, searching for bullet casings. Caro saw Gerry with new eyes that night; she thought he looked adorable in his black tactical pants and long-sleeved base layer. Gerry watched Caro's ass each time she bent over to plant an evidence flag. They went out for coffee at 7 a.m. Then, in the back of Gerry's van with the blacked-out windows, they had hot and passionate sex. They went home and slept for a few hours separately. They had sex again that night. A month later, Gerry moved in with Caro. She started having the best orgasms of her life. One orgasm after another, after another, after another.

"Leave the shower on for me!" Gerry called out from bed.

As the bathroom filled with steam, Caro thought she'd like to raise the topic of babies, marriage, and buying a house together. It seemed like the right time, but then maybe it was too soon. They'd only been together for a month. Caro defogged the mirror with her fist, stared at her almond eyes and Roman nose, and thought, *I hope the baby gets my eyes and his nose. Gerry has a cute nose. I don't want a baby with my nose.* She was ready for domestic life. She wanted to be a wife and a mother, especially if the package came with a daily orgasm. As she left the mirror and walked to the shower, she resolved she'd talk to Gerry that night about babies, marriage, and looking for a house in a nearby safe suburb.

She lifted a foot over the rim of the shower, she was about to step under the rush of water, when she stopped. Her eyes arrested on a spot on the wall. There, on a tile that was eye-level, just outside the shower, a long, black hair stuck to the wall. One end of the hair came loose with the shower breeze. It fluttered before her. *That's not my hair,* she thought. *It's too long and shiny, and thick around the root to be my hair.* She grabbed a set of tweezers from behind the mirror. She plucked the hair from the tile and held it against a corner of toilet paper. *The only people with keys to the apartment are me, my landlord (who is bald), the landlord's wife (who has red grey hair), and Gerry. Gerry has a key now.*

Caro heard Gerry outside the bathroom. She heard his heavy feet hit the hardwood floor. She lunged for the cabinet under the sink, snatched a Ziplock bag full of travel shampoo and soap and scrunchies—dumped everything on the floor—and stuffed the black hair wrapped in toilet paper in the Ziplock bag. The door slid open and there was Gerry, staring at her. Caro was breathing hard, her body was contorted, her breasts were against her knees. Her head was upside down and filling with blood. She gathered miniature soaps and travel shampoos and scrunchies off the floor.

"What the hell are you doing?" Gerry asked.

"I'm getting in the shower," she lied.

-

Caro's friend Rebecca looked up from thirty pounds of drug powder spread over a metal table. They were in the lab in the basement of the police precinct. Rebecca, young and pasty-skinned with dark bags under her eyes, worked too many hours. *Lab ghoul* is what Gerry called Caro's friend behind her back. Caro had told him Rebecca was once cute, bright-eyed, and sexy, but forensic work had stolen her looks. Now all she did was work, eat, work, eat, take sleeping pills, barely sleep, volunteer for night shifts to avoid not sleeping, work and eat and work more, in that order.

"What do you want me to do with this hair?" Rebecca asked.

"Can you test it?" Caro whispered.

"Test it for what?"

"—ID it."

"I can't ID it. Not without a case number," Rebecca said.

"I can give you an old case number," Caro suggested.

"I'm sure you can. But that's against the rules. And anyway, look at the hair sample. If the root isn't attached, I can't do anything with it."

"Come on," Caro goaded. "Please?"

"Please what? You want me to risk my job for a hair you picked off your bathroom tiles? What do you think is going on here?"

"Well—" Caro paused and thought about whether to lie to Rebecca. But it was no use. Rebecca was smart. "—If Gerry invited a girl to my place and they had sex in my shower, I should know about it. Plus, this hair will give me an exact ID, and I can look the girl up on social media. I can see what kind of person she is."

"If you think Gerry brought a girl to your apartment to have sex with, in the first month of your relationship, it doesn't matter what kind of person she is. You know what kind of person *he is,* and you shouldn't be dating him."

"But I like him. And I could be wrong," Caro said.

Rebecca turned her gaze away from Caro. She picked up her metal scooper and went back to work, scooping, sorting, dividing piles of brown powder next to her microscope.

"Please ID the hair, Rebecca. I just need to know." Caro pulled the sleeve of her friend's white lab coat.

"We've been here before," Rebecca said, low under her breath. "You did this with Christopher."

"I did not."

"And Nico. And Rob. And that guy from the Stamford Police Department. You always come to me with the same fantasy—that this guy is different for this and that reason, and that he's amazingly shaped and he'll be an incredible husband and dad and breadwinner and he's in it for the long haul and he's an athlete and he's religious and all the rest of what you're looking for. Then you bring a hair or nail sample, or I can't remember what you brought with that guy from the Stamford Police Department—was it a condom? Then we go through this, again and again and again. You delude yourself into thinking you found someone *other* than your type, then you prove that nothing has changed."

"That's not true—" Caro started to defend herself.

"Rebecca!" a voice boomed from the doorway. Sargent Calabro, 250 pounds of old-man muscle in a stained uniform, eating a biscuit taco with chunks of neon egg spilling out, stood there, blazing impatience from his eyes. "I see thirty pounds of meth and coke unsorted and unlabeled, and two girls gossiping like it's a day at the beach," he said, pulsing his eyes from Rebecca to Caro.

"Please?" Caro whispered to Rebecca.

-

Caro sat in her ski jacket at her big steel desk in front of a clunky computer. It was May, it was eighty degrees outside and sunny, yet the air-conditioning in her office blasted so hard that the tip of her nose was cold. She had a foot heater under her feet. She opened a chat box on her computer and typed with frozen fingers:

10:32 a.m., *Hey. Do you remember that guy Gerry D. from College Point?*

10:32 a.m., *Hi Caro! How are you? What's new?*

10:32 a.m., *He was in C block with you.*

10:32 a.m., *Okay. Hang on. Let me find a pic.*

10:32 a.m., *Do you know if he was a good guy? Was he trustworthy?*

10:32 a.m., *I recognize his face. But I don't know him.*

10:32 a.m., *But do you know if he was like, a dick? Or a sleaze? Or disgusting?*

10:32 a.m., *I honestly have no idea.*

10:32 a.m., *You sure???*

10:32 a.m., *I really don't know him. Hey, by the way, how are you? Want to grab dinner sometime? I haven't seen you in ages.*

10:33 a.m., *Is there anyone else you can ask? That was in C block?*

-

Caro sat on her bed watching an old season of *CSI*. Her back was against the headboard. Her legs were folded tight to her chest.

She hadn't gotten a positive ID on the hair from Rebecca or received any news from her friend in C block at College Point. The issue still burned bright in her mind. Gerry was about to come home from work, and she didn't know how she should act toward him. She was still in the first inning of her suspicion, and she could call off the game. She could pretend to be a loyal, loving, unsuspicious girlfriend with no special knowledge of what he did in his free time.

She heard the front door to the apartment open. Gerry threw his heavy boots against the wall. He appeared in the door to the bedroom, looking very cute. He crawled onto the bed next to her. Without a word, he pried open her knees. He moved his head down her leg and fumbled with her zipper.

"They wouldn't use a cotton-tipped applicator there. They don't even know it's blood. It could be rust or chocolate sauce, dirt . . ." Caro said to the TV.

"Hey, babe?" Gerry said. "Can you help me out here?"

Gerry's hand was snaked under her shirt, he was undoing her bra, and she pretended to be totally engrossed in the *CSI* rerun. Because now she wasn't sure if she had the mental restraint *not* to mention the hair she found that morning.

"Can I ask you a question?" Caro blurted.

"Huh?" was his response.

"Gerry, why did I find the hair of another woman stuck to my bathroom tile?"

There, she'd said it. She'd made a big, leaping assumption, and she couldn't take it back now. She saw his shoulders tense. He rolled off her and onto his back.

"What are you talking about?" he asked.

"Why was there a long, black, shiny hair stuck to the wall?" Caro asked.

"I have no idea. I have no clue what you're talking about." He swung his feet to the floor. He rose and went with heavy legs to the door.

"Where are you going?" she called out.

"Food," he grunted.

-

Caro leaned against a rack in the evidence room. It was quiet in this room at the station, and she needed time to herself. They'd had a big fight. He'd claimed over and again that he had "no idea" and "no clue" to what hair she was referring, but he refused also to go into significant detail of his activities that week. He refused to be audited, judged by her, when he'd done nothing wrong. He'd acted as a loyal, loving boyfriend. He didn't want to be put through the wringer for no reason. Now, because Caro wasn't satisfied with the rebuttal he'd offered, she was deep into Gerry's Facebook page on her phone. She was looking for clues as to who he'd spoken to and where he'd been that week. She was going back through the week, the month, the year; if she had time before Calabro came back, she'd go further back into Gerry's social media feeds.

"What are you doing now?" Rebecca asked, moving past her with an armful of evidence bags.

"I'm combing through every one of Gerry's social media feeds. Looking for clues."

"You confronted him?" Rebecca asked.

"Well kind of," Caro said. She thought about how to phrase Gerry's defense. "Gerry said he has no clue what I'm talking about. I think he could be telling the truth. But *I can't confirm he's telling the truth.* You can help me out. If you ID the hair, I can come up with a theory."

"A theory?" Rebecca asked.

"Sure, like, the hair stuck to the wall when my landlord brought someone into the apartment to clean or repair something. Or it came through a vent from another apartment. Or it flew into an open window. Remember that murder on Lexington and 59th Street? Defense attorneys showed that the hair, the single damning piece of evidence, could have floated from the head of a stranger on the subway, up the subway shaft, into the apartment shaft and into the apartment. That kind of thing happens all the time. Or maybe Gerry brought an ex-girlfriend or cousin, or his mom or something into the apartment for a secret family tragedy reason, and he doesn't feel close enough to me yet to tell me why he did this."

"Caro?" Rebecca said. "Have you considered dropping the issue?"

-

That night when Gerry fell asleep watching *The Late Show* on mute, Caro crept out of bed. She took his phone into the bathroom and tried to unlock it. After five attempts, she failed and was locked out. She went back into the bedroom and put his phone back on the bedside table. *Gerry's nose looks adorable,* she thought. *I hope our baby gets his nose, and maybe his blond, fuzzy hair.* She lifted his black tactical pants off the floor. She went through both pockets, removing a receipt, a parking stub, gum capsules, two lint balls. She photographed everything so she could study it the next day.

-

After two laps of the block outside the police station and several calls to her mother—who wasn't picking up, Caro decided she'd
ask Gerry a follow-up question. She risked angering him. She knew
this. But then she'd found things on his social media feeds that she
couldn't quite explain. She'd found a receipt from a Tex-Mex restaurant: margaritas, chips, wings, with a time stamp of Tuesday night.
Tuesday night he'd said he was working. She didn't want to get into
another drawn-out, passionate, terrible fight. She didn't want to
upset him. Her hands hovered over the keyboard. She'd ask him a
question, he'd answer it correctly, and that would be it. She'd move
past this little volcano in their relationship. Before she typed, she
wondered, just briefly, if she should *not* do this on her work e-mail.

1:12 p.m., *Hey. Gerry. Are you there? Can we talk?*

1:12 p.m., *What's up*

1:12 p.m., *I know I asked you this, but did your ex-girlfriend have
long black hair?*

1:13 p.m., *Gerry?*

1:15 p.m., *Gerry?*

1:19 p.m., *You can't be serious right now*

Caro sat at her desk, staring at her screen, wondering what else
to type. Should she have not asked that question? The black hole of
insecurity opened inside her. She'd been on a good path with the

whole thing, but now maybe her assumptions and accusations were too acute. Maybe she'd gone too far.

-

"I'm sorry about everything. I totally believe you," she whispered to Gerry across the table in a dimly lit bar. After a lot of tears, negotiation, and missed calls, he'd finally agreed to meet her for a drink. But now that they were face to face, she could see his coldness, his indifference bordering on disgust. She was on thin ice with him, she knew, and if she said one single word he didn't want to hear, he'd get up and leave.

They sat for two drinks, then a third, and she was afraid to open her mouth. She'd done herself the favor of wearing a low-cut silk shirt that showed the top of her bra. As the music in the bar shifted from hip-hop to soft jazz, she saw him looking at her breasts. This was good. This is how she'd get back into his good graces.

"Caro," he said. "I want to go home with you. I really do. I just don't want you to accuse me of things I haven't done." He reached his hand across to touch hers. "Can you trust me, please? Can we drop this? Once and for all?"

Caro felt her heart collapse in her chest. *I love him. I don't want to lose him,* she thought. *I need to push this out of my head.*

-

That night, as they had sex, Caro clamped her eyes shut. She couldn't look at his face—the nose and eyes that usually turned her on—because every time she looked at Gerry, she could only see him burying himself inside another woman's vagina with shower water crashing down on them.

-

Seven days of peace and quiet passed. Her visions, suspicions, and twisted fantasies gave way to a period of calm in the relationship. Caro received a call to work a crime scene in lower Manhattan one sunny morning. As she rode the ferry across the Hudson River, as the sun twinkled on the water and a soft wind played on her cheeks, she decided she'd ask Gerry about marriage, babies, and finding a house in the suburbs.

She deboarded the ferry, walked along the promenade outside 300 Vesey Street—she was deciding whether to walk or call a ride-share to get to the crime scene, when she stopped short. There was the Tex-Mex restaurant. The green-and-white awning fluttered quietly, innocently in the wind. All the tables were empty this time of morning, but she could imagine it. She could see Gerry sitting at a table on the outer perimeter with a view of the boats in the harbor, eating wings with one hand, slipping his clean hand onto the leg of the woman across from him. Maybe that was the woman he'd fucked in her shower.

-

The next morning, Caro got her period. She felt it an hour before the alarm went off, so Gerry was dead asleep when she went into the bathroom. She sat on the toilet and reached into the sink cabinet for a tampon. Her head was a few inches lower than normal. She was reaching low and to the side—when she saw it. Her gaze arrested on the base of the toilet. There, stuck in the grout, between the toilet and the floor, was a pubic hair. She *couldn't not* inspect it. She grabbed her tweezers. She plucked the pubic hair from the grout and held it out against a corner of toilet paper. She studied it from every angle.

-

"No. I refuse to do this," Rebecca said.

"Please? Come on. Help me put this issue to rest. At least tell me if it's a match to the first hair I brought you. Tell me if the pubic hair matches hair from the scalp. You don't need a case number to confirm or deny a match. *You can help me out with this one tiny thing.* You're not breaking a department rule by helping me out," Caro pleaded.

Rebecca left the metal table in the lab. She exited through a set of heavy double doors that led to a sunken parking lot. Caro followed her outside.

Now they were in an outdoor bay in the parking lot adjacent to the police station, and in front of them was a badly decomposed body. The body was wrapped in a purple shower curtain that still had the shower curtain rings attached. Rebecca started pulling a white hazardous-material suit over her lab coat. She stopped, considered her shoes, and then resumed getting dressed. She snapped on protective glasses. She picked up a power washer.

"I don't want to be part of this," Rebecca stated.

"You're not part of it. You're acting as a friend," Caro said.

"Friends *help* friends. This isn't helping you. It's making you a lunatic," Rebecca said.

"Come on, please, Rebecca," Caro goaded.

"And by the way, a week ago you said everything was great between you and Gerry. You'd found religion. He wasn't a liar, cheat, and asshole. He was the perfect man. But now we're back to square one. He's a liar, cheat, and asshole again. Which is fine, you have the right to change your mind. But I want to be left out of the process. I'd like to cancel my subscription to your issues. I won't risk my job over it. I won't ID the pubic hair. That's it. No. I'm done with this baloney," Rebecca said, dropping the hose onto the corpse. She turned her back on Caro and walked away.

-

She had everything prepared. When Gerry came home from work that night, Caro was in a baby pink camisole and nothing else. She'd dimmed the lights in the front room of the apartment. Several candles were lit. An open bottle of chilled chardonnay was on the table. There was a glass bowl of ice with microbrew beer on top. Crackers and pimento cheese. Soft classical music played. A smile spread across Gerry's face, wide, bright, unflinching, as he took in the scene. He acknowledged what Caro wanted tonight, and he was into it.

"I love this," Gerry said, reaching for Caro's waist.

She let him hold her, smell her neck, run his hands down her side. They had a few drinks, snacked a little, nuzzled, cuddled. They even rolled around on the floor. She waited until he started to peel the last of her lingerie off.

"I love you, Gerry, I love that you live here, I love our sex together, I love everything about our relationship. I want you in my life. I want to have a baby together. But I need to ask you something. I know it's going to upset you, but I can't leave the issue alone. I need to know so we can move on with our lives," Caro said.

Gerry had his face in her breasts. He wasn't happy she was speaking.

Caro continued, "I found a pubic hair on the base of the toilet yesterday. It took me a while to find someone in the lab who would help me ID it. But I did ID it. I matched it to the other hair I found stuck to the shower wall. It belongs to a woman. I know who the woman is, but I want *you to tell me why that woman was in my bathroom.* There are plenty of reasons you could have invited her into my apartment. But I'd like an explanation. I deserve to know why she took a shower in my bathroom and sat on my toilet. Did you have sex with her? Did you not have sex with her? I want to know. I need the truth from your lips."

Gerry finally met eyes with Caro.

"Are you seriously doing this again?" Gerry asked.

"I need to know," Caro said.

"Fine," he said, crawling away on his knees. "I want you to know, you're going to be alone forever," he said. He laced up his boots and left.

As the door to the apartment swung shut, Caro dropped her head back on the hardwood floor. She looked down at her camisole, the flickering candles, the chilled wine. She listened to the music for a few beats and then decided that she'd masturbate.

-

On the hottest day of August Rebecca called Caro down to the basement of the police precinct. They were at the metal table and there was a dead Rottweiler laid out with evidence tags next to it. Caro stood off to the side, getting distance from the stench, as Rebecca swabbed blood globules from the dog's nasal cavity.

"Can you make this quick? It smells like hell in here," Caro said.

"Look at my phone," Rebecca said, tossing it across the table.

"Why?" Caro asked, sensing an apology in Rebecca's tone.

"Just look at it," Rebecca said. "That's Love Salazar's Instagram account. She got married last week in a church in the Bahamas to a guy named Gerry D. Do you happen to know him?" Rebecca smiled. "Anyway. I took the liberty of going back through her Instagram account to April and May of last year, and guess what I found? Tons of pictures of Gerry and Love together. While he was living in your apartment, sleeping in your bed, eating your food. Anyway, I don't mean to upset you with this, but I thought I'd offer it as an olive branch. You were right. I'm sorry. But I'd like to repeat my original advice. *Don't pick lying, cheating, freeloading losers.* Don't date them. Don't invite them to live with you. Just don't do it."

Caro scrolled through the photos, feasting her eyes on Love Salazar's long, beautiful tresses. She had black, shiny hair with thick roots. Her wedding dress was off-white lace and very small, two inches above the knee. The dress was cut in a heart shape around her perky tits. Gerry looked radiant. In every photo, he kissed his new wife, or cradled her shoulders or lifted her into his arms. There were endless opportunities for Gerry to show his affection for his new, sexy wife. Finally, when Caro had gorged herself, made herself sick with pictures of the two of them in matrimonial bliss, palm trees and confetti and champagne and friends in string bikinis in hot tubs, she threw the phone back to Rebecca.

Rebecca was back in her focus zone, bent sideways with a six-inch Q-tip stuck deep into the dog's nostril. There was a blood sample she couldn't reach.

"Question for you," Caro asked.

"What do you need?" Rebecca answered.

"Can you look at something for me?" Caro dropped a Ziplock bag onto the table. Rebecca looked up, the smile fading from her face.

"I met a cute guy at a bar last week. He's living with me now. Rob is amazing, he's smart and funny and strong, and well, he's everything to me. But I found this on the bottom of his shoe . . ."

Chapter Five. Slip-and-Fall

It was fiscal year-end and there was one claim sitting on her desk. Claim 616. The claim was incomplete, unfinished, unresolved, marked "pending investigation" since the day of the slip-and-fall accident. No matter how many times Wendy James reviewed the file and combed each detail, she couldn't make a judgment.

Should she refer it to the fraud department?

That year, she was a claims investigator working in an oatmeal cubicle with tackboard walls on the seventh floor of a brown glass office building in Wayne, New Jersey. She hated her job and worse, she hated the landscape of her job. The view from her desk led to ribbons of freeway. In the distance, commuters floated by in their metal boxes moving from home to work or the gym to work and home and work and the gym again, with a stop at the gas station or grocery store, in the same grim, miserable, physically exhausting pattern that Wendy knew each day. The whole affair was tedious. Depressing and soul draining. Wendy hated her work at the insurance company. She loathed suburban, corporate drudgery.

I rue the day I left the FBI, she thought, as she dragged her hi-liter over a section of Claim 616 that seemed suspicious. Under PLAINTIFF STATEMENT there was a blank spot. A big hole. When an agent on the floor below had called the plaintiff, Evelyn

Egan-Jackson, single, Caucasian, age fifty-six, for a statement describing the accident and injuries, the plaintiff had refused to speak on a recorded line. Then she'd given the name and phone number for her lawyer as if she was expecting and anticipating a fight with the insurance company.

Power move, she wants the upper hand on us, Wendy realized darkly, as she scanned the other sections below PLAINTIFF STATEMENT. There were too many details left missing. Blank, unfinished, incomplete. Under the section REPORTED INJURIES it simply said, "shattered hip" and "torn knee ligament." *Those aren't medical terms*, Wendy noted in her notebook. Combing through the rest of the hard data, or lack thereof, Wendy's stomach soured. There was nothing, zilch, zero contained in Claim 616 that put Wendy's conscience at ease.

As the morning dragged on, Wendy's thoughts clouded over. She went to the bathroom and stared in the mirror. Every day, no matter how much bronzer she wore, she could see tiny lines appearing on her forehead. Her outfit—a fast-fashion tweed skirt and jacket, only $89, paired with a white silk shirt with breastfeeding stains and two-inch black mules, un-chic but functional shoes—did nothing to lift her appearance. Or make her look younger. Wendy believed that she wore her thirty-two years badly. There was no reason to reapply lip gloss. In the mirror, she appeared lifeless, dead, missing.

She returned to her desk and studied the file.

This claimant, Evelyn Egan-Jackson, a tall, lumpy woman—she confirmed it by looking at the photographs—was probably the type of woman who filed claims regularly and expected the insurance company *not* to ask questions. Now she'd filed a major, serious, claim, and if she succeeded in her pursuit she'd win $1.2 million from the Zurich-based parent of Wendy's employer, Empathy Claims.

And yesterday, hell, Wendy wouldn't have cared. Why should she care? She was a prisoner in this office park with mulch dividers and red zinnias sticking like tumors from the grass. She counted the minutes between when her workday was over, when she could drive her Chevy Blazer with plates that read SNIFFR—a joke gift from her husband—out of the parking lot and onto the highway, she counted the minutes she slept and ate and watched TV, before she had to return for the next workday. She followed those idiots with neon-green plastic badges into the turnstiles in the lobby. The pharmaceutical people in green badges who shared the office building were sad, scary robots who were exploding civilization without breaking a sweat. Wendy worked next to them. The more she thought about her distaste for her day, this place, for every person who worked in this office park, everything around her—everything she could see and smell and hear—the more Wendy realized she couldn't take another minute of this existence.

Why did it feel life her life was ending?

Before motherhood and marriage had conspired against her, Wendy had been in a great mood. She'd been a pioneer. She'd graduated top of her class at Quantico and started a blistering career at the FBI. Her investigative work on an insurance fraud scheme led to one of the largest prosecutions in New York State. Bill Constantine. Bill Elephant. Arnold Dowd. Those three fraudsters, two personal-injury lawyers and one orthopedic surgeon, conspired to steal $31 million from small businesses and insurance companies before Special Agent Wendy James brought them to justice. Wendy *herself* had brought the whole shebang, evidence upon evidence upon more evidence, proving these fraudsters were guilty, to the desk of the U.S. Attorney. The jury deliberated for a total of seven minutes. Mainly, primarily, it was Wendy's ravaging investigative work that got written up online and in the newspapers.

But now, she could barely remember her success.

With a sigh, Wendy reached across her cubicle and picked a booger someone had stuck to the brown grainy plaque on her wall: CLAIMS INVESTIGATOR.

Domestic life had swallowed her whole. At thirty-two years old, she went from FBI team captain to breastfeeding stinking babies by night and sleepwalking the halls of an insurance company by day. As the sad movie of her life played in her head, she thought, *I'll never again be Special Agent Wendy James at the FBI. I'll never carry a gun to work. I'll never lead a life of high stakes and adrenaline. Most likely, I'll rot and die processing insurance claims in this oatmeal cubicle with tackboard walls and a view of the freeway.*

Evelyn Egan-Jackson's ugly mug stared up at her.

-

After lunch, something stirred in Wendy's soul. She didn't know what it was about this woman and her fried blond hair and ruddy cheeks, her claim for $1.2 million—but it lit up a part of Wendy's prefrontal cortex. Some primitive force in her bloomed. There rose a feeling, an intuition, a clairvoyance—that if she could do something with this claim, if she could *prove* something to someone about this claim, if she could produce right from wrong and justice from injustice and honesty from corruption—she'd feel alive again. Maybe, just for one second of her day everything would go back to the way it was when she'd liked herself. Here was the call, the opportunity, the narrow, dark, winding road to self-respect.

But what could she do with the claim?

Her iPhone alarm erupted into birdsong—1 p.m. was her first allotted post-lunch coffee break—and Wendy rose from her desk. This wasn't going to be easy. She'd stretch her legs and get a cup of free iced coffee from the cafeteria. She'd take it downstairs and outside and loop the parking lot until she figured out a plan. If she needed a second cup of coffee—hell, even a third cup of coffee—she'd go back inside and get one. She was going to solve the mystery of Claim 616, even if it overcaffeinated her and kept her awake all night.

Suddenly, she was up from her cubicle, moving swiftly down a row of cubicles toward an oatmeal-colored elevator. Her focus was deep when a squeaky voice pierced the air.

"Wait up up up! I'm coming with you!"

-

Helena Velasquez, rounding forty, boarded the elevator next to Wendy. Helena was a tall, bug-eyed woman with a haircut that only a teenager should have. Shaved sides and hedgehog bangs. Her jean spaghetti-strap dress revealed a red lace bra that matched her red plastic clogs.

"Hey, you," Helena said coyly. "Can I come with you?"

"Hey. Sure," Wendy answered flatly.

Normally, Wendy would have eschewed Helena's company. Wendy judged Helena to be an annoying person who lacked personality. When Helena made sex jokes, it was because she had no other way to capture people's interest.

"Want to hear a joke?" Helena asked.

"Not right now," Wendy said. "Because I'm working out something in my head."

"What are you working on?" Helena asked with a coquett-ish smile.

"Right now? I'm working on Claim 616," Wendy stated.

"What's so great about Claim 616?" Helena asked.

"It's a slip-and-fall, and it's suspicious as hell," Wendy said.

"Did you refer it to the fraud department?" Helena asked.

"No," Wendy said bluntly.

"Why not?" Helena asked.

"Because. Well. I'll tell you why. You know, back when I was an FBI agent, I uncovered a $31 million slip-and-fall scheme committed by three fraudsters. Bill Constantine. Bill Elephant. Arnold Dowd. Two personal-injury lawyers and one orthopedic surgeon. You might have read about it online," Wendy said.

"Sure. Everyone knows about that case," Helena said.

"Did you know that I was the investigator who uncovered it?" Wendy bragged.

"That's impressive," Helena said admiringly.

Helena batted her eyelashes at Wendy, and, surprisingly, Wendy didn't mind it.

Wendy continued. "So, today, I'm sitting at my desk looking at Claim 616 and I have this realization. It hit me like a bolt of lightning. I don't need to send this claim to the automatons on the third floor. I can do the work myself. I'm capable. Claim 616 is full of gaps, holes, issues, irregularities, peccadillos. It's a trap that Empathy Claims shouldn't fall into. This woman is the worst kind of rent seeker. She wants $1.2 million for an accident that statistically, in all probability, didn't happen the way she describes it. Or not to the severity, the intensity, the degree to which she feels entitled to claim compensation. I finished right near the top of my class at Quantico. I delivered a $31 million fraud case on a silver platter to the U.S. Attorney's

Office. Why would I outsource this work to the fraud department? I can process this claim myself."

"I bet you can," Helena encouraged her.

"Exactly!" Wendy nearly shouted.

The elevator was traveling swiftly through the bowels of the building. Wendy fell back into deep concentration. Helena tipped her nose forward.

"Hey, you want to know something about me? I wasn't always an initial claims processor. I used to work on the third floor. In fact, *I worked in fraud* for six years before I moved upstairs," Helena said.

"You did?" Wendy asked.

"You bet I did. I know a lot of things. Maybe I can help you," Helena suggested.

When Wendy didn't answer right away, Helena skewed her eyes to the floor. Wendy decided there was something lovable about Helena's deep insecurity.

"You know what? If you have a background in fraud, if you think you can help me with elements of this claim, then I'd love your help. The more the merrier," Wendy said.

"Terrific!" Helena yelped. "You make my day!"

The elevator doors opened to the twelfth-floor cafeteria. The women made a beeline for the free coffee station, preferring not to look around. The dining area was once a hub bub of activity inside the building. A piazza. A town square for coworkers to meet. A sunny spot to drink soda and read your phone. But now, because so many Empathy Claims employees had been laid off or reduced to part-time or work-from-home, the cafeteria was all but decommissioned. It was not staffed. It was not supplied. Furniture was stacked against a wall. The hot-food stations were deserted. Where mounds of neon-yellow eggs and rubbery French toast once lay, occupying metal vats, there were heat lamps pulsing down on nothing.

"Let's get our coffee and get the hell out of here," Helena suggested.

"Parking lot?" Wendy asked, filling her takeaway mug.

They boarded the elevator again and hit L for lobby. Helena stood on the same side of the elevator where Wendy stood now. Wendy enjoyed the camaraderie. She felt optimistic about the partnership. If Helena really had a background in fraud detection, their work together on Claim 616 could be fruitful, productive, dynamic.

"You know what the first rule of fraud detection is?" Helena asked as the elevator shot down through the building.

"Give it to me," Wendy said.

"That sounds sexual—" Helena smiled, paused. "Okay, here it is. The first rule of fraud detection is magic three. We need three pieces of proof, three columns of solid evidence before we can make an accusation."

"Hmmmm…." Wendy mused.

-

For their loop around the parking lot, Wendy regaled Helena with battle stories from her days at the FBI. She described her zenith moment: Bill Constantine, Bill Elephant, and Arnold Rude being read their rights.

"You should have seen the look on their faces. They never imagined they'd get caught. It was one of the greatest moments of my life. I'm sorry if I'm boring you," Wendy said.

"You're not boring me! Tell me everything!" Helena cried out.

"—well, the part I haven't told you is that these men abused their professional licenses and fancy degrees to screw the most vulnerable members of society. The people they recruited for their slip-and-fall scheme were drug addicts and homeless people. It was Elephant's idea to walk into methamphetamine clinics and ask these people—desperate, pathetic humans—to cross a crosswalk and fall into a pothole. Or trip on a crack in the sidewalk. Or tumble down a cellar opening outside a fast salad restaurant. Constantine was the mastermind on locations; he picked the best accident locations in the five boroughs. After the victim tripped or slipped and collapsed, after he sustained said 'injury' he was whisked uptown to 76th Street and 1st Avenue to the office of an orthopedic surgeon named Dr. Arnold Rude, who performed medically unnecessary surgeries and charged exorbitant amounts. Elephant and Constantine, the personal-injury lawyers, would take it from there. They filed claim after claim—$31 million was divided three ways between these men! They were buying Lamborghinis. Ferraris. Jet skis. Lake houses!" Wendy nearly shouted.

"You know, you're really something," Helena said, admiringly.

Wendy couldn't remember the last time she'd received praise from anyone, and it was making her face feel warm. She found herself telling more stories, searching for ways to impress Helena. Wendy then stopped and pointed to her car, a gold Chevy Blazer with plates that read SNIFFR. The windshield was baking under the sun.

"You know that's my car?" Wendy asked.

"Yeah?" Helena asked.

"—and I have a secret," Wendy blurted out.

"What's your secret?" Helena asked, her eyes alight.

"On my last day at the FBI, I wanted a souvenir. So, I slipped into the munitions room and put one in my bag. A big one. I don't even have a license for it, but I keep it in the glovebox of that car," Wendy said. She made a trigger motion with her hand.

"You *stole* a gun from the FBI?!?" Helena covered her mouth and silent laughed.

"Does that impress you?" Wendy asked.

"Wow…" Helena said. "I can't believe how my day has turned around."

-

Helena's cubicle became ground zero for the investigation. It was not a tidy place, it was covered in 7-Eleven detritus—Lay's chip bags, vape pens, 5-hour Energy shots, and rows of crusty nail polish bottles—but Wendy liked it better than her own cubicle. There was good energy at Helena's desk. It was nice to have their chairs crammed together. The portable fan made a low *whirring* noise, and the Chinese cat clock waved at them.

The work went quickly.

Wendy stated, "Evelyn Egan-Jackson wants $1.2 million for a shattered right hip and torn knee ligament. These injuries are the result of a slip-and-fall accident that took place inside the guest cottage on the property of Shelly R. Lazarus of Alpine, New Jersey… yada, yada…"

"Who is Shelly R. Lazarus?" Helena piped in.

"A wealthy woman that Evelyn worked for. Let's investigate that part," Wendy said.

"Where is Alpine, New Jersey?" Helena asked.

"A wealthy town where the wealthy woman lived. Evelyn claims she was doing a job for her at the time of the accident. Let's investigate that part too," Wendy said.

"Should we enlarge this photograph?" Helena asked.

"We should enlarge all of them. Let's ask the graphics department to show us every inch of Egan-Jackson's body, every angle of her fall, the tile, the edge of the bathtub, the hip bone puncturing her skin. Let's get it all mega-size, close-up. Also, we should ask the graphics team if *they see* anything shady, fishy, irregular, or dubious about the photographs Egan-Jackson submitted to Empathy Claims," Wendy said, thumbing the file.

"Remember, we need three pieces of evidence," Helena said.

"I remember," Wendy said.

After lunch, with the newer, enlarged photographs, they made a timeline of the accident. Wendy laid the 8 x 10 photos in chronological order—beginning of accident to middle of accident to end of accident. The first frame revealed Evelyn Egan-Jackson lying there like a beached whale on bathroom tiles, white bone sticking from her leg. The second frame showed the paramedic arriving and pointing to Evelyn's hip injury. Then there was a photograph of Evelyn, in anguish, as she's loaded onto a stretcher and rolled into the back of an ambulance. Evelyn, being wheeled into the hospital. Evelyn posing against an interior brick wall in a billowing hospital gown, looking freshly post-op drugged. The Physical Therapy Center. Evelyn, looking determined, as she's fitted for crutches and knee and hip braces. Evelyn pointing out her new, inconvenient life. Home desk. Home bedroom. Home kitchen. All of it freshly outfitted with pulley systems and rubber mats and foam guards to prevent Evelyn from reinjuring herself. A shriveled woman, a nurse or aide, evidently hired at great expense to help Evelyn navigate her new life. The last set of photos was taken inside the Physical Therapy Center, where the light was blurry, grainy, blue greenish. Evelyn on the long road to recovery. Evelyn Egan-Jackson doing four kinds of squats. Sumo squats. Barbell front and back squats. Single-leg squats. Her right hip and her bad leg are supported by foam blocks in several pictures.

"There's so much here that looks suspicious. Honestly, I don't even know where to start," Helena said.

"Let's start at the beginning," Wendy said. "The morning of the job. Did she enter the bathroom and loosen a tile *before* the slip-and-fall occurred?"

-

By the close of the next business day Wendy and Helena had built their case against Evelyn Egan-Jackson. They were so thrilled with their work, the list of deceptions, falsehoods, libels and inaccuracies, misrepresentations and deceitfulness—they'd proven there was no way the accident could have occurred the way it was described, nor cost what Egan-Jackson claimed it cost in her out-of-pocket itemization report—Wendy and Helena were so pleased with their progress that they photocopied Claim 616 and took it with them, to celebrate, at a nearby fast-food sandwich chain.

It was 5:30 p.m. The sun blasted down on a red plastic picnic table. As the women unwrapped sandwiches from wax paper, the conversation drifted.

"Do you really keep a gun in your car?" Helena asked, gazing at Wendy's gold Chevy Blazer parked nearby.

"I have condoms and cigarettes too," Wendy said conspiratorially.

Helena opened her mouth in a silent laugh, and Wendy could see chewed up deli ham and foamy bread on her tongue.

"Want to hear a disgusting joke?" Helena asked.

"After," Wendy said.

"After what?"

"After we call Evelyn Egan-Jackson to confront her," Wendy said.

"Shouldn't we do that tomorrow at the office? On a recorded line?" Helena asked.

"Fuck the recorded line," Wendy said, picking up the claim file.

Wendy scanned her notes, mouthed words silently, preparing herself for the call.

"Are you sure we should do this here, now?" Helena asked.

"I've never been surer in my life," Wendy answered.

"Fine. Here's her phone number: 555-217-4002," Helena said. "By the way that's an Oregon number. Bonus if you can tell me why *this woman* has an Oregon number."

"It's the only state where insurance fraud is not prosecuted as a crime?" Wendy whispered, as the phone started to ring. Helena winked. Wendy held her breath, waiting for Egan-Jackson to answer.

"Hello, who is this?" snapped a hostile voice.

Wendy sat up.

"Hello. Good evening. This is Wendy James from Empathy Claims calling—" She paused and cleared her throat. "—I'm trying to reach Evelyn Egan-Jackson. Do I have Evelyn Egan-Jackson on the line?"

"Yes, this is Evelyn."

"Do you have time to discuss the claim you submitted?" Wendy asked.

"Do I have time? *I've waited months* for your call," Evelyn said.

Wendy could hear the anger in Evelyn's voice. She wasn't going to give this woman any chance to advance. She summoned her authority.

"Well, I'm calling today because I need to speak to you about your accident claim. But first I need to verify your identity. Can you provide your Social Security number, home address, birth date, and pass code for the claim? Also, I need to inform you this is a recorded line. If you're interested in filling out a survey at the end of this call, you'll be prompted."

Evelyn, irritated, rattled out the information.

Wendy softened her tone. "I need to tell you, Evelyn, we've identified several problems with your claim. There are issues, holes, gaps, and irregularities that we can't account for. Quite honestly, we need you to choreograph the accident again. We require evidence that these hospital bills, physical therapy bills, are *real*."

"Excuse me?" Evelyn barked.

"Just what I said," Wendy shot back.

"Did you say you need evidence the hospital bills are *real*?" Evelyn asked.

"Well—" Wendy hesitated. Helena pinched her leg. "Yes. That's exactly what I said."

There was a long, unnerving silence.

"Can you give me your full name again?" Evelyn asked.

"Can I give you *m-my* full name?" Wendy stuttered.

"Yes. I've been paying insurance premiums to your company for a decade now. This is the first time I've ever had a major accident. I've just gone through the worst year of my life. I'm in serious pain. I provided every shred of documentation Empathy Claims required. I even hired someone to help me compile the expenses, itemize the report, and today—tonight—is the first time I get a response from anyone at Empathy Claims. Now you tell me you aren't sure if I suffered this injury or spent my life's savings or missed a year of work? Spell *your* full name," Evelyn stated, coldly.

Wendy gulped. "W-E-N—"

When Wendy finished spelling her name, the line went dead.

The two women sat at the plastic picnic table, scattered with smelly sandwich remains. The wind picked up and knocked over a soda cup. The mood was decidedly low.

Helena tried to cheer Wendy up.

"What do a vagina and a cigarette have in common?" Helena asked.

"I dunno," Wendy said, looking glum.

"The closer you get to the butt, the worse it tastes."

-

The next week was torture. Wendy wasn't sure what course of action she should take; should she tell her supervisor about the call with Egan-Jackson? Or should she continue to build the case against the hostile claimant, and wait until she was confronted? Wendy sat in her cubicle, in a low-esteem outfit, her silk shirt covered with breast-feeding stains and her brown mules, the leather scuffed on the heel. One morning, her nerves were so on edge that she slipped vodka into her coffee.

"I think you're forgetting something," Helena said, leaning on the wall divider. "You have her dead to rights. She's not going to call our boss. She's not going to call anyone at Empathy Claims. She's probably five states away by now, filing another fraudulent claim at another insurance company. Praying she doesn't get caught."

"Agree to disagree," Wendy said.

"Seriously? What happened to your confidence?" Helena asked.

"I don't know. I know I'm right about Claim 616, but I'm not sure that anyone will believe me," Wendy said.

"What about all the great work we did?" Helena asked.

They debated back and forth like this for days.

Once, when the claustrophobia of the situation was too much, when Wendy couldn't take her cubicle anymore, she went outside for fresh air and leg movement.

"I'm going outside," Wendy said.

"Can I join you?" Helena asked.

"I need a minute alone. To think. I'll be back in ten minutes," Wendy said.

Outside, the office park was hotter than Hades. Heat waves rippled off the asphalt. Wendy leaned on the side of her car for a while. Then she decided the sun on her skin was dangerous, so she retrieved a baseball cap and dark sunglasses from inside. She was reading a magazine under the shade of an elm tree on the parking lot divider, when it happened.

A black, unmarked Ford Explorer crawled into the parking lot.

Right before her eyes, Evelyn Egan-Jackson stepped out of the car.

From twenty feet away, Evelyn was imposing. She was tall and large and muscular. Evelyn's white billowing sundress revealed her huge, rippling shoulders and thick legs. Wendy sucked in her breath as the plaintiff locked her car, turned to the brown glass building and approached the entrance. Evelyn was walking toward the lobby of Empathy Claims, she intended to go inside. Wendy knew, she needed to stop her.

"Hey you! Evelyn!" Wendy shouted from under the tree.

Evelyn turned and looked.

"Do I know you?" Evelyn asked.

Wendy approached Evelyn. It dawned on Evelyn, that Wendy was the agent she'd spoken to about the claim. Now, as Wendy stood close to the claimant, she liked her even less than she had on the phone. She could see Evelyn's bad facelift, she could smell her flame-grilled blond hair, the hairspray caked onto her scalp. Evelyn wore fake eyelashes; they were big black things, basting brushes, that stuck out past her nose.

"I'm Wendy James, we spoke earlier," Wendy said with gusto.

"Let's get this over with," Evelyn said, pointing to the lobby.

"What are you talking about?" Wendy asked.

"The meeting. At 3 p.m. Your supervisor said—"

"You called my supervisor?" Wendy asked, barely hiding her shock.

"My lawyer has spoken to three people at Empathy Claims this week. I'm surprised you don't know that. Anyway, I'm going inside," Evelyn said, ambling off.

For a beat, Wendy watched Evelyn move away. She could smell the vice, the sleaze, the venality, and deception. But self-discipline kept her from acting. *Don't do it, Wendy. The art of war is not to engage in war. You learned patience, control, restraint at Quantico. You give into your impulse, you go down this path, and anything can happen. No one can pull you back. Close your eyes. Breathe.* Discipline held her. *Phew.*

Then out of nowhere, anger rose in Wendy's throat.

Evelyn Egan-Jackson, the woman who'd filed a claim for $1.2 million she didn't earn and didn't deserve—this parasite—was headed inside Wendy's workplace. She was going to complain bitterly about Wendy's aggression. She was going to get Wendy fired from Empathy Claims, and then Wendy would have a hell of a time describing why it all happened the way it happened to future employers. Wendy's fury grew thick. Her vision twisted. She felt bile rising from her stomach. She wanted to kick this woman to the pavement and wring her neck. Or beat her with a dull object. Or stuff the claim file full of lies, gaps, and issues, right down her throat and suffocate her. She wanted to teach this perverted degenerate a lesson.

"You motherfucker—" sounded from Wendy's throat.

Wendy shuttled toward Evelyn and struck her hard, across the shoulder blades.

"What the *fuck*?" Evelyn cried out, in horror, toppling to the ground.

Wendy started raining down blows on Evelyn's shoulders, back, and neck. She shouted into her face, "—Tell this to your lawyer!" and "You're a liar, a cheater!"

Evelyn was bleeding now. She was reaching, grasping for something in her bag.

"Do you know I've put insurance schemers in jail?" Wendy shouted.

Evelyn finally got inside her bag, opened it, and lunged at Wendy. She had a taser gun pointed at Wendy's neck. Wendy saw the weapon—and sprang away. Wendy wasn't fleet of foot, but she was faster than Evelyn. She sprinted through a column of parked cars, hopped the divider. Evelyn followed, chasing her with the taser gun. When Wendy hit a hydrant accidently, when she tripped and stumbled forward, Evelyn overtook her. She punched Wendy and squashed her face in the mulch. She held the taser gun, ready to drive it into Wendy's face. Wendy kicked and squirmed, twisting out from under Evelyn's bulk.

"You'll regret this!!!!" Wendy yelled.

"Fuck you, woman—" Evelyn spat in her face.

Wendy held her clicker out, she *beeped beeped* and sprinted toward her Chevy Blazer. She was inside the car, reaching for the glovebox when someone pulled her by the legs. She was dragged back onto the pavement.

"WENDY! STOP! STOP THIS!" Helena cried out.

"It's her fault. She's dangerous!" Wendy shouted and pointed.

"STOP. STOP THIS. Everyone is in the conference room. Let's all go inside. We can settle this like professionals," Helena pleaded.

Wendy was panting. She was glad to see Helena. She gripped her hand and looked up over her shoulders. There was clear, blue sky overhead. The leaves of the elm tree rustled. The highway traffic sounded like a river rushing by. For a minute, she felt calm. *The worst is over. I confronted Egan-Jackson. I did my job.*

"Okay. You're right," Wendy muttered.

Just then, Evelyn rose like Medusa. She was behind Helena. Her white sundress was splattered with blood. Her lips and gums were bright pink. One of her fake eyelashes was severed, dangling in her face. "You psychopath motherfuckers—" she hissed.

Before Wendy could stop it, Evelyn knocked Helena flat to the pavement. A blur of violence followed. The three women toppled, tumbled, kicking, slapping, punching each other across the yellow parking lines. Evelyn screamed. Helena came up for air. Wendy crawled away to get repurchase. Slaps, kicks, punches, choking, elbow to the windpipe, knee to the neck, more screaming, more yelling, spitting, coughing, attack followed by détente, followed by attack and attack and attack and more blood. The punches, slaps, kicks, tossing, and tumbling continued. Finally, a dark-haired fifty-year-old man with a neon-yellow badge emerged from the dark glass doors of the lobby. He had called the police. He was capturing the fight on video. The blood and hair and skin of the three women was starting to loosen, smear, spread around. Cries, groans, guttural sounds pierced the air.

Screaming police sirens.

"Those women! Right there, officer!" screamed the fifty-year-old supervisor. The first police officer climbed from his cruiser with a knowing look.

"You're under arrest. All three of you!" the police officer shouted through a horn.

-

Six months and a day later, Wendy, Helena, and Evelyn stood in pink paper hats and pink cloth jumpsuits emblazoned with a patch: PEF Community Service, Inc. They had aluminum pickers in hand. They were picking trash off the side of a two-lane highway. Litter-strewn grass lay behind and in front of them, as far as the eye could see. Wendy plucked up a flattened soda can. She held it with her picker. She debated whether to drop it in her shiny garbage sack.

"You know, I've been thinking," she called out.

"What?" Helena and Evelyn called back in unison.

"Constantine. Elephant. Rude. Those men collected $31 million in insurance reimbursements from their slip-and-fall scheme before anyone was the wiser. They bought Lamborghinis and Ferraris and lake houses. They pled guilty to every count of insurance fraud, wire fraud, and mail fraud, and do you know how much prison time they did?"

"How much prison time?" Helena asked.

"None," Wendy said.

"None?" Evelyn asked.

"Supervised release," Wendy said. "And they forfeited *less than ten percent* of their earnings. I calculated it after the whole thing was finished. In fees and fines they paid $971,000, $1.2 million, and $475,000, respectively."

"That's it? That's all they paid the court?" Evelyn asked, her interest piqued.

Now the three women in pink jumpsuits moved about, pickers suspended, while a warm breeze blew past, feathering trash over the road.

Their brains moved in unison.

"You know… if we work together, who says we can't be the next Constantine, Elephant and Rude?" Wendy turned around. A smile ignited her lips.

Chapter Six. Mr. Wang

During the fall of 2012, I lived in faculty housing at John Jay College in New York City. I was a new student, so it was by administrative error that I'd been left off the freshman dormitory roster and put on a list of visiting professors. So it was, I moved into a tall townhouse in the west 50s, with diseased ivy crawling up the brown bricks and in between the aluminum frame windows. The first-floor kitchen and library were helter-skelter places; visiting professors came and went and left behind whatever they'd purchased while they were there and didn't want when they left. Cheap coffee makers. Coatracks. Melamine laptop stands. Books. Bad subway art. In the study, there were several TVs and no remotes. Mostly, I kept myself to a single room at the end of the hall on the second floor where I could live and study in the afternoon light that snuck across 8th Avenue. As often as I was invited, I went upstairs to visit a professor, a disabled man, who I still think about today.

His name was John Yung-wen Wang.

I guessed Wang was about forty-five. He had a slab of black hair that fell into his eyes, and a smooth, perfect scar cutting vertical-style through his left eyebrow. He wore thick hearing aids, pressed blue jeans, and always a white shirt under a red or blue silk frog-button jacket. As a kid, he'd broken his right leg and a rural doctor had botched the operation. An infection impaired his hearing. Because of his infirmity, he needed help climbing the stairs of the townhouse and walking around outside. At John Jay College, where he taught Chinese political science to a sold-out lecture hall, he kept a walker next to the podium. He was wildly popular among his students; his course was audited by students and faculty who had no specific interest in Asian Studies. They came to hear him speak.

Always, in his lyrical way, he wove his life experience into the coursework. He explained to students who didn't know enough about Mao Zedong's rule that during the time he grew up in China, the population was emerging from one of the worst periods of suffering in history. His own parents were political dissidents, they were jailed, one was shot. He lived in an especially poor part of the country with distant relatives who didn't want him, especially with his disability, and wouldn't feed him if he misbehaved. He wasted some of his youth, his potential, scavenging for food and shelter. This was dangerous but also fun. At seven years old he ate a rat for breakfast, at eight years old he worked in an iron-smoldering factory, and at twelve he met a band of corpse walkers who knew one of his parents from jail. He walked to the neighboring province with them. In his teenage years, he made enough money selling pornographic magazines that he was able to move to the city and fight his way into a real education. By hook and by crook, he ended up at Tsinghua University in Beijing. That, he told everyone, was a minor miracle. It changed the trajectory of his life forever.

Wang's students loved to hear him tell these stories, they loved his vulnerability and his disposition. When they found out that I lived at the same address as Wang, I became popular. Friends followed me home. We'd climb upstairs and knock politely on Wang's door. If he wasn't writing—he was producing a 550-page tome, a definitive history of the "Gang of Five"—he'd invite us inside to sit on the big brown futon in his room.

Wang always had cello music playing. His sitting room was cluttered with gifts from his many visitors. Professors from other colleges, diplomats, new and old friends, students who wanted to win his favor, they all brought him something. Cut tulips in a jar, painted figurines, dragon-beard candy, burnt-sugar peanuts, hand-drawn cartoons, poems, playbills, maps of sightseeing in New York, interesting stamps and coins and foreign currency, dog-eared books, foreign-language magazines and newspapers, red wine and white wine and rice wine, whiskey, pens, red glossy envelopes with Broadway theatre tickets. These gifts lay in piles. It was fun to thumb through the items as Mr. Wang talked. Wang was immeasurably kind and generous; often he encouraged me to take anything I wanted.

I wasn't his only admirer in the house. The pair of resident advisors, thirty-something pink-haired sisters, doted on Mr. Wang all day and night. They brought breakfast right to his room, and tea, and snacks from specialty stores. They took his towels and bed sheets to be laundered at the place he liked far downtown. In the afternoons, they'd alternate taking him outside for fresh air and exercise. Often, the sisters would squabble over who took him on his walk to the Hudson River Parkway, where he liked to see the Intrepid. Sometimes, if they couldn't settle the argument, the three of them would go arm-in-arm together. One sister on either side, supporting Wang.

I noticed that the sisters also acted as Mr. Wang's personal concierge; they accepted mail and packages. They printed documents for him. They received visitors, of which Wang had many. Every time I left or returned from class, one of the sisters was headed upstairs to give Wang something. Wang was grateful for the assistance. He never stopped thanking them for what they did to make his life easier.

Only once did I see him irritated.

It was completely my fault. I was up wandering the townhouse at 3 a.m. because there was a decision on my mind, and I couldn't sleep. I heard tinny music coming from his room—it was different from the usual cello music. A soft light crept from underneath the door. I thought, for some reason, that he must be awake grading papers. Or finishing a chapter of his book. I knocked softly. The door was unlocked, so I pushed it open.

I immediately realized my mistake. Mr. Wang was half-naked at his computer, humping, jerking, moving up and back and sideways with his erect penis cupped in one hand. There were two young women on his laptop screen. One woman's tongue hung from her mouth while she held her flat-brimmed cap. The other woman, in a pink fuzzy costume, pressed her nipples to the screen. They were all singing an anthem song, but when they saw me, they stopped singing. The tinny music blared. Wang jolted from his chair. He swung around and pointed a sharp thing, a letter opener, in my direction. Cold, hard confusion was on his face. He pretended he'd never seen me before, didn't know me, as if I were a stranger crossing into his dream. His hearing aids were not in his ears, and I wondered if his senses were scrambled. The screen went black, and as I backed out of the room, Mr. Wang began to cry. I was so angry at myself for trespassing, for embarrassing him deeply, that I didn't go upstairs again to his room for weeks. I avoided him to the best of my ability.

Eventually, I worked up the courage to apologize. "Mr. Wang, I'm so sorry. It was a mistake. I entered your room when you weren't expecting me," I said.

"It's okay," he answered. Mr. Wang was warm and gracious. He told me not to worry about it. The intrusion meant nothing. It was water under the bridge. To my relief, he invited me to sit on his brown futon again. After that, we talked the afternoon away. We ate snacks and enjoyed an expensive vodka that his Polish friend had brought. Sadly, I told him, it was my last week living in the townhouse. The administrative error that landed me in faculty housing had finally been corrected. Soon, I would move to a student dormitory on 118th and Amsterdam. My life would center there since it was so near the lecture halls and cafeteria and gym and library. Upon saying goodbye, I promised him that I would visit as often as my schedule permitted.

Months later, I received an unexpected job offer from the State Department, a four-month contracting gig that took me out of the country. I didn't return to classes until the following year, and it wasn't until early December, on a freezing-cold day, that I rode the N/R train down to the theatre district and walked several blocks west to visit the brown brick townhouse where Mr. Wang lived with visiting faculty.

One of the pink-haired sisters was outside the townhouse, cleaning the front steps. She was in a shiny puffer jacket, with her scrub brush in a bucket of soapy water. "How is Mr. Wang?" I asked her. "Is he here? Can I go upstairs to visit him?"

She shook her head no. Then she stood there looking disheveled and sad. "You didn't hear what happened to Wang?" she asked me.

"What happened?" I asked, alarmed. As she explained, I heard defensiveness in her voice.

"Believe me. We called the campus police as soon as it happened. As soon as we figured out that he was missing. I went to his room one day with his breakfast—and he was gone. Just gone. His closet was cleaned out. His desk was swept clean. Not a single item, nothing, on that coffee table in front of the couch. None of his stuff was in the bathroom. His tests, papers, that leather bag he took to class, it wasn't there. It was all gone, no imprint left behind. Maybe he was in a bad way. He just left and disappeared . . ." Her voice trailed off.

"Strange. In his condition?" I asked.

"Yeah, that's what we said. How does a man who needs hearing aids, who can't walk around the block by himself, just disappear?"

-

Ten years pass. It's early October 2022. I'm on special assignment in Beijing, China, which is closed to visitors. I'm on a State Department visa, three days expired. I intended to visit a friend outside the capital, but I can't get there. I can't get anywhere, in fact, because a national holiday is underway. No buses, cabs, trains, or planes are running. All transportation is suspended. To leave, I'll have to wait until the national holiday passes.

As I walk to the military parade a few blocks from my hotel, I feel uneasy. Unsettled. I should stay in the hotel room, read, eat, sleep, and watch TV, but I'm stir crazy. I left my documentation in the room. From my experience with Beijing authorities, it's better to explain no documentation than the wrong documentation.

As I approach, I see it's a full-blown military parade running down Chang'an Avenue. The energy is incredible. Thousands of grandparents, parents, and children who have been cooped up in their apartments for months spill out onto the streets. They line the sidewalks, cheering, waving, to enjoy the music, the spectacle of this holiday, *Shi Yi,* or Ten One, the day the People's Republic of China was founded. Beijing looks different. The sky is crystal clear overhead because the factories have been shut off for a week. The loop road is silent. White, puffy clouds drift over Beijing's sparkling glass skyscrapers. I walk up and down the parade line, snapping photos to show my friends at home. Some 15,000 military personnel, 160 aircraft, and 580 pieces of weaponry move together in one direction.

In the excitement, I forget myself. I move past a group of children clutching red balloons, dancing on their tiptoes, and crane my neck to see the action. Across from me, there's a tank-shaped object hidden under a green blanket. Next to it is a wall of black-clad guards.

The guards are taking orders from their leader.

My eyes arrest on the older man; he's in a long black wool coat, olive flat-brimmed cap, and a handsome black scarf. He has a scar cutting vertical-style through his left eyebrow. I study his leg and see that it is strong and straight. He stands tall and moves perfectly.

Before I can flip my head, he feels my stare and looks directly at me. There's a parade between us—I have time to move, to disappear—but I don't. I'm frozen. Because he's looking at me with something like recognition, friendship, longing. As the parade music rises to a deafening level, I realize I've made another mistake. Mr. Wang smiles at me, and somehow I know I'm in danger.

Chapter Seven. My Month with Bjornstein

I had terrible stomach cramps the night they came for Bjornstein. I'd drunk a bottle of Maalox between 10 p.m. and 2 a.m., which was the first time I'd done that in my life. You see, I have a strong digestive system. I'm not the type to get food poisoning or suffer bouts of diverticulitis, diarrhea, or gut cramps. But that night in August of 2019 I suffered blinding abdominal pain. I spent the night shuffling from toilet to bed, bed to toilet and back again. Heaving, gagging, retching water. Losing fluids. Sweating, oozing, leaking brown and yellow and green liquid from the other end. I was emitting terrible noises through my anus. For hours on end, I leaned against the wall. I mopped my forehead with a lukewarm washcloth. I lay flat on the tiles, then I perched on my knees, then I tried to walk off the pain. Toilet to bed and back again I went, all night long. Finally, I got on my knees and prayed to the porcelain gods that I would not pass out. There was a lightning rod of pain connecting my lower ribs to my bowels. I prayed and prayed and prayed that I would not pass out from the pain and miss the 6 a.m. bus to the Metropolitan Correctional Center at 150 Park Row in the Civic Center of Lower Manhattan.

I needed to get to prison. I couldn't miss my bus.

That summer, my charge was Henry Bjornstein. He was in a Manhattan jail awaiting trial for a crime that made all his famous friends cringe and wince. Forcible copulation. Sexual assault. The trial was set to begin in August. It was a big deal in the press because everyone knew Henry Bjornstein. He was a rich and connected man. He'd had a big career. He consorted with British royalty, Hollywood, Wall Street, and the White House alike. He'd committed sins. But he had every resource to hide those sins until he didn't. Now here he was, like Job facing an angry God, and no one knew why his hour had come. No one knew what would happen to him. Least of all, me.

I was an eager and fervent young man that summer, a newly minted U.S. marshal. Bjornstein was my biggest assignment to date. I'd moved to New York City specifically for the job. I was squatting in my sister's Cobble Hill townhouse basement, paying my share of electric and water and streaming cable, which went to waste because I worked so much. I spent sixteen hours a day if not more looking after Bjornstein. The prison was severely understaffed, and the security measures they installed were not up to our standards. So it was, I was there all day and most nights, sending reports to my boss in Atlanta. My job, to serve the federal judiciary through the protection and transport of a federal prisoner, was as high-stakes as it could be that summer. My boss told me repeatedly not to screw this up. The eye of the world was upon us. The risk that something would happen to Bjornstein was growing by the hour.

"Just get that man to trial," my boss told me when he assigned me the job. "He's hated. Despised. Reviled by everyone. They want him dead."

I wasn't sure who the "they" was he was referring to, but I'd heard rumors like everyone else. When Bjornstein was originally assigned to the third floor, cell 3E, when he arrived in his clean white jumpsuit, blue eyes alight, his face freshly washed, his shock of white hair standing up electric-style, he frightened everyone. One of the guards took one look at him, walked right into the warden's office, and requested a transfer. "I don't want to be near him," he whispered to me on his way out. The inmate across the hall, awaiting trial for double murder, had the habit of masturbating when anyone passed him. Even he, who typically snarled and spit, convulsed, gripped his piece, was silent as Bjornstein got settled in that day.

I could see it with my own eyes. The prison was afraid of Bjornstein.

There was a cloud of unease, anxiety, fear, disquiet, apprehension, and alarm—panic—that followed him everywhere he went. The commissary lady told him not to visit her window. The lice checker refused to comb his hair. The cafeteria workers kept a wide berth, never getting near his table. The warden didn't visit the third floor once while Bjornstein was there. The janitor wouldn't enter his cell. There were blood and urine stains on the wall directly outside, and the stains stayed there against protocol. Every morning I'd arrive to work and complain. There Bjornstein would be, alone, reading in his bed or in front of the frosted window. He was as calm as if he were reading on his back porch at home.

I'll say this now. I didn't mind Bjornstein. He talked a lot to me, and not about prison issues. He talked about literature. Philosophy. Math. Since I was the only person who took him to the caged roof area for recreation, the only one who struck up conversation with him—we formed a rapport. He liked me and I liked him.

Once, he told me he was left-brain dominant. Logical, orderly, analytical. Until he got to prison, then out of nowhere, he began having visions and dreams. One day I escorted him to a pretrial meeting at the courthouse, and he talked to me about mythology and symbolism. He told me that if you dream that someone is chasing you and your legs are too heavy to move, if you can't run or leap or climb or get away, it means something. It means you haven't done your work in this lifetime.

"Did you have that dream last night?" I asked him.

"I dreamt about a mountain in Beersheba. It's a desert mountain made of sand and loose stone. I was in a long white lab coat and my feet were cut up. The sun was burning my skin off. When I got to the top of the mountain—it took me all day to reach the summit—an angel appeared and said August 15."

"August 15?" I asked.

We were in the subterranean tunnel that connects Metropolitan Correctional to the federal courthouse. We were about to meet his defense attorneys and the U.S. Attorney.

"August 15 they will come for me," Bjornstein said. "I don't know the hour."

Initially, I didn't know what to make of his pronouncements. For several days, I didn't relay this information to my boss in Atlanta because I didn't know exactly what I'd say. Or how I'd say it. How could Bjornstein know anything about his fate? Even the people in charge of his outcome—the attorneys, the presiding judge—were in heated argument over details of the trial. Who would be allowed to testify against him? What evidence would be admissible? What type of sentencing was reasonable? Would bail be revisited?

"Your lawyers are fighting hard for you," I said to Bjornstein one day when we were upstairs in the recreation zone, the caged-in rooftop of Metropolitan Correctional. Bjornstein loved it up there. Through the barbwire he could see blue sky, sunshine, and the Manhattan skyline with its sparking spires.

"They won't get me out of this," Bjornstein said.

He was jogging around the perimeter, from one corner of the rooftop to the next: north to east to south to west.

"They have good arguments. They could lighten your sentence," I said.

"It will be over on August 15. You'll see," Bjornstein said, turning the corner and peeling off. For an older guy, he was quick on his feet. His white jumpsuit flapped in the wind as he sprinted ahead of me.

The next morning, the guard station was deserted. The lens of one of the cameras outside cell 3E was smashed. Shards of glass were on the floor. No one had picked up anything. I found Bjornstein curled up on the floor five feet from his bunk, he was in the fetal position, and he was concussed. He had a clear pool of vomit next to him. When I lifted his body and shook his shoulders, he was hazy, foggy, and confused.

"What happened? Did you hit your head?" I asked him.

"They came for me. But it wasn't time," Bjornstein said.

"*Who* came for you?" I demanded.

"Last night. I told them about my dream. I was climbing the desert mountain and the sand kept shifting below my feet. My lab coat was getting pulled down, caught, eaten by spiders and seaweed. At the top the angel told me to wait until August 15," he whispered.

I went outside and made calls. Protocol dictated that I call for medical attention. I was hesitant to relay specifics, because the last thing I wanted was for the prison doctor to refer my charge for psychiatric help. I knew Bjornstein had been attacked by someone. I could see that the person who attacked him made it look like self-harm. Or suicide.

"I've got a problem here," I whispered to my boss in Atlanta. I was three blocks south of Metropolitan Correctional. I'd gone to a coffee shop to make the call in private. "Someone tried to hurt Bjornstein. They made it look like he tried to do it himself," I said.

"How do you know?" my boss asked me.

"Because I know. I know what an attack looks like. I know what self-harm looks like. He didn't try to hurt himself. Someone smashed the camera outside his cell, which is further evidence that he was attacked."

"Maybe he smashed the camera," my boss said. "Or actually, that doesn't make sense."

We went back and forth, debating the topic. I had to get off because someone was urgently trying to get a hold of me. It was a 917 number.

"What's going on?" I asked a third-floor guard named Ray V.

"You might want to come back. They're taking Bjornstein to a psychiatric facility in the Bronx. I've never heard of the place."

"I'll be right there. Don't let them leave," I said.

I sprinted all the way back to Metropolitan Correctional. I had to argue my case, fight my way inside the armored van that was taking Bjornstein uptown. He was muzzled. Secured to a metal stretcher. Surrounded by two male doctors with iPads. One was young, tall, blond. The other doctor was older, in a back brace.

"I'm the U.S. marshal in charge here. I go everywhere with him," I told the young doctor.

"He's going for evaluation," he said.

"I'll accompany him," I demanded.

The older doctor turned to me. "They won't let you inside the room while he's being evaluated. That's the rule. No exceptions will be made."

"My job is to get this man to trial. Nothing and no one will stand in my way. If you'd like, I'll put you on the phone with my boss at the U.S. Marshals Service. He has a direct line to the attorney general. I'm sure the attorney general would love to talk to you," I said.

The doctors conferred with each other. Then they nodded to me. I climbed into the back of the medical transport, where I stood against the wall. I kept an eye on Bjornstein's lips. The entire way up the West Side Highway, I made sure he was breathing. He took gasps of fresh air. Then he started muttering.

"Are you okay?" I asked.

"Get me *The Misfortunes of*—" Bjornstein said.

"What do you want?" I repeated. I didn't understand what he wanted.

"Public Library. *The Misfortunes of Virtue,*" he managed to say.

We were passing into the underground parking garage of the psychiatric clinic. I stood back against the wall of the medical transport. I waited for the staff to unlock the doors and unload the stretcher. To my surprise, a totally different set of doctors opened the doors and took us into a tunnel which led to the facility. The younger, blond doctor and older doctor with a back brace were gone. In their place was Dr. Sanderson, her hair in a severe black bun, black suit, white canvas shoes. She introduced herself as "chief clinician" and told me she would lead Bjornstein's evaluation.

"I'll be in the room while you do the evaluation," I said.

"That won't be possible," she said.

"I represent the federal judiciary. You can take it up my boss in Atlanta," I said. I handed her his card. Then Dr. Sanderson put us in a waiting room with white concrete walls and mauve floor tiles. There was a framed photo on the wall. It was a photograph of the moon, its craters and mountains. Bjornstein studied it with awe.

"Please come with me," Dr. Sanderson said when she returned.

The evaluation room was as big as a conference room. It was not equipped to handle prisoners; in fact, none of the normal security measures were installed. I wanted to check my phone to see if this psychiatric facility was even mentioned on the Bureau of Prisons website—if these were certified Bureau of Prisons psychiatrists—but there was no internet service inside the room. I went outside to the hallway, and still I couldn't get service.

Dr. Sanderson invited another clinician, Dr. Ernesto, a man with dark pencil-thin eyebrows into the room. They asked me to arrange Bjornstein so he could sit up and face them in his chair. As I removed his arm and leg restraints, they didn't seem nervous.

"I'm armed," I reminded them.

When I secured Bjornstein into his chair, as he faced the doctors across the conference table, there was a flicker of light in his eyes. Recognition? Or déjà vu. Did he know these people? Had he met them before?

"Are you ready to begin?" Dr. Sanderson asked Bjornstein.

He nodded quickly.

"Last night, you were found on the floor of your prison cell. We believe that you are in danger of hurting yourself. These are standard questions. Please answer to the best of your ability," she said. Then she began. She drilled questions. Dr. Ernesto recorded responses into his plastic-covered iPad.

"Do you have thoughts of hurting yourself?"

"No," Bjornstein said.

"Do you think about death or dying?"

"No."

"Do you think of harming yourself?"

"No."

"How many times have you tried to harm yourself or take your own life?" she asked.

"I haven't," he answered.

"When was the most recent time?"

"I didn't try to hurt myself," Bjornstein said calmly.

"When were you most serious about suicide?"

"I can't answer that," he said.

"Why can you not answer that?" Dr. Ernesto wanted to know. He raised an eyebrow.

"I did not try to harm myself," Bjornstein said.

"When was your most serious attempt at taking your own life?" Dr. Sanderson persisted.

"Never," Bjornstein said.

"Can you explain that?" she asked.

"I didn't try to hurt myself," he said.

"How do you feel about your own future?" she asked.

"I see it clearly," Bjornstein said.

Now, the two doctors left the room and compared notes. I could see them through the chicken-wire window. They appeared to be finished with the evaluation. They came back inside and said they would need another hour to prepare follow-up questions for Bjornstein. I checked my watch. I went outside to call the warden. We were due back at Metropolitan Correctional by 5 p.m. Prison rules. I was concerned about rush-hour traffic on the West Side Highway. When I returned, I reminded the doctors that we were on a strict schedule. They needed to wrap up the evaluation. Dr. Sanderson told me she had more questions to ask before she could make a final recommendation. Then she turned to Bjornstein and started talking again.

"Sometimes people feel their life is not worth living. Can you tell me how you feel about your own life?" Dr. Sanderson asked.

"I feel optimistic," Bjornstein said.

"What are the aspects of your life that make it worth living?"

"Books. *The Misfortunes of Virtue. Insomniac Dreams.* Music," Bjornstein answered.

Dr. Ernesto noted this response on his iPad.

"Do you ever wish for a permanent escape from life?" she asked.

"Once," Bjornstein said. "In a dream."

I was surprised by this answer. He'd done so well avoiding their accusations.

"Was the dream last night?" Dr. Sanderson asked.

"No. It was last week. I dreamt I was climbing the tallest mountain in the Negev desert and the sand kept shifting below my feet. My lab coat was getting pulled down, caught, eaten by spiders and seaweed. At the top of the mountain the angel told me that on August 15 I will be delivered. The angel didn't tell me the exact hour."

Now both doctors, Sanderson and Ernesto, studied their subject with great intensity.

"Okay, then, we'll wrap up," Dr. Sanderson said.

Swiftly, they left the room. We moved Bjornstein back into the medical transport. Just as I suspected, we battled heavy traffic all the way back to Metropolitan Correctional. By the time we arrived, the warden had the psychiatrists' recommendation. He pulled me into his office and delivered the bad news.

"They want him moved to a special housing unit," the warden said, handing me notes from the evaluation.

"Henry Bjornstein is not suicidal," I said.

"They want him on suicide watch. It's the safest thing."

"Safe for who? For you?" I asked.

I was fuming. Bjornstein wouldn't be safe in a special housing unit. It was an open secret that the ninth floor was the most precarious place in the building. Prisoners there were under twenty-four-hour surveillance, but the floor had its own code, procedure, and protocol, which meant that anything could happen.

Immediately, I made calls. I called my boss, who called everyone he knew at the Justice Department and FBI, trying to get the decision unwound. Before dinner, Bjornstein was moved upstairs to the ninth-floor special housing unit. He was not allowed any personal items; he was forced to leave behind his toothbrush, paperback book collection, his extra white jumpsuit and sneakers, his orthopedic pillow, his towel. He was put in a cell with no roommate. The only guard there, an ancient beast with sunken eyes, brown dentures, and orange curly hair, sat in the shadows. He never left his chair.

When I went up later to visit Bjornstein, to console him, he was looking at the corner of his cell where the window used to be. There was no window there.

"I'm sorry this happened," I said.

"Don't be sorry. You did everything you could," he said.

"My job is to get you to trial," I said.

"It's an impossible task. It's not your fault," he said.

I'd come here to console him, and now he was consoling me.

"Maybe if you hadn't said that last part about your dream and the angel, they would have submitted a different recommendation. They didn't like that part," I said.

"It doesn't matter," he said calmly.

"You shouldn't keep talking like that. If you think bad, dark thoughts, just keep it inside. Don't say it out loud. They are recording every word you say. They will use it against you. If you act normal and positive and optimistic, if you show good behavior up here, they'll move you back to 3E in a few days," I said.

Bjornstein smiled weakly.

When I left Metropolitan Correctional that night, I fought the urge to call and check in every fifteen minutes. I tried to stay optimistic. The night air was cool. My head felt clear. It was good for me to take a break from work. I needed to step away from the intensity of the job I'd been assigned. I needed food. I stopped at a noodle stall on Fulton Street. It was a place I'd never visited before, and a young attractive Vietnamese lady smiled at me and said I'd love a spicy soup. I stood on busy, chaotic Fulton Street and slurped my noodles. For the first time that day, my stomach was full. I felt happy.

Thirty minutes later, I had to sprint off the bus and squat behind a dumpster to release diarrhea. I barely made it back home to my sister's apartment. I crawled through the door and went straight to the toilet. For the next three hours, I felt abdominal pain like I'd never felt. Satan was in my stomach. I drank Maalox and more Maalox, until I'd finished the whole bottle. I retched and spewed and expelled, churned out brown and green and white liquid, I ejected onto the carpet and tiles and my own bedsheets. I plunged the toilet at one point. I vomited. Around 4 a.m., closer to 4:30, I passed out from pain. At 6:25 a.m., I awoke with a start, realizing my mistake. I'd missed the bus. I was late.

As I sprinted into work that morning, I had a barrage of notifications on my phone. Something had happened. People were trying to get a hold of me.

It was too late when I got there.

Bjornstein was curled into a ball ten feet from his bed. There was a ring of purple bruises on his neck. "No pulse," someone declared.

Intense discussion followed. No one knew how to handle this. Were we investigating suicide? He was in a suicide unit. But it was clear he'd been attacked. Everyone inside the cell, anyone looking at his body, could see that. There was the bruise pattern on his neck. The way he'd been dropped on the floor. He was clearly concussed. The surveillance camera outside the cell had plenty of footage, but it was blacked out, scrambled. The only guard, the ancient red-haired guy had left for his break at 3:43 a.m. He'd come back at 4:14 a.m. He'd signed the log, certified his absence. He had no idea what happened to the prisoner.

Someone offered a theory that Bjornstein hung himself, strangled himself with his bedsheet. His suggestion was so ludicrous, we ignored him.

"What the hell did you eat last night?" another U.S. marshal asked me when I took another trip to the bathroom. There was nothing left inside my body. I was sick, pale, emaciated and needed to lean against a wall for support.

"Bad noodles. I lost five pounds last night," I admitted to him.

He leaned in and whispered, "So *who* do you think did it?"

I felt like lurching again. I needed fresh air, space, a place to breathe. They were starting to prod the cadaver, swab evidence from his skin. I couldn't be near the investigation.

"Can we get a positive ID on the teeth?" a detective asked as I left.

As I took the elevator down, I heard inmates on other floors of Metropolitan Correctional cheering. I heard their whoops and hollers and cries and stomps. The news was spreading. As I exited security and passed onto the sidewalk outside the prison, the walls started to shake. It was a celebration. Cameramen started to arrive.

Three days later, I flew to Atlanta. I was in the waiting area outside my boss's office when the first headline hit: "Bjornstein Strangled Himself."

Within the hour, I was assigned to another job in Dallas.

The internet leaked bits and pieces of information. I checked for updates, insight, new angles on the events surrounding Bjornstein's death. I was curious what details would be shared, and what parts would be withheld. I was surprised by a lot.

They published a list of items the feds had confiscated from Henry Bjornstein's townhouse apartment. Passports. Cash. Jewels. Priceless art; a row of individually framed eyeballs; a six-foot-tall naked African warrior sculpture; a John Dubuffet painting; a Persian carpet; *Woman Holding an Opium Pipe Caressing a Snarling Lionskin*; a nine-foot ebony Steinway "D" grand piano; and the stuffed black poodle from a Paris flea market valued at $725,000 that stood on the top of the piano. Rare, first-edition books. When I saw a title, *The Misfortunes of Virtue*, I remembered something.

And now I should say, as a U.S. marshal, I took an oath of secrecy. On top of that, I signed a stack of nondisclosure forms regarding "official information" around Bjornstein's death. I was warned several times not to answer questions or speak to the press. I was notified by a lawyer for the Bureau of Prisons not to comment on the investigation.

But I'll say this.

I went to the New York Public Library. I found a window bench in a small archive room. I followed Bjornstein's directions and found the exact edition of the exact title he asked me to find. Inside the back cover, I ran my finger across a row of numbers scribbled in pencil. 76318-059. Yes, that was the inmate number they'd assigned to him on his first day in federal detention. Underneath that number, in pencil, the date August 15 was scribbled. Then the hour. Then the minute. Everything he said to me about his end was true. It was there in pencil. I closed the book and put it back on its shelf. As I rose, I could see a patch of blue sky through the window. I thought of Bjornstein on the roof of the prison, smiling at the clouds.

Chapter Eight. Diary of a Prosecutor on the Run, Part II

The night I crossed the Piscataqua River Bridge that connects Portsmouth, New Hampshire, to Kittery, Maine, the fog was thick. I had my windshield wipers at full speed and my dehumidifier on high, but the visibility was terrible. Patches of light and dark fog turned to sleet, mist and back to fog. I slammed my brakes. There was a car stopped in the middle of the highway, spun sideways to avoid a truck that was blocking two lanes. My breath caught in my throat. My nerves turned ragged. I was sleep-deprived and my vision was starting to blur. I'd left New York City after midnight and driven into the early hours of the morning. Every assurance I gave myself— *I'm doing the right thing. This will all turn out in my favor. Nick and Lila will understand*—felt like a lie.

I had the number for John Haas, my CIA friend, on a napkin in my pocket. I had the vague outline of a plan in my head. I was headed to John's house in Deer Isle, where he lived on a compound at the end of a spit of a land. I'd drive there. I'd present myself in person and ask him the question, *How do I do it? The defendant's assailants are following me. How do I protect myself, buy cover? What steps do I take?* As I followed a row of dark evergreens up the exit ramp, as I left the highway for a winding country road banked in mist, the thought occurred to me, *Maybe I should call him first?* But how would I do that? I'd disabled my phone. Just then I passed a small gas station. I couldn't remember the last time I'd seen a public payphone. But there one was. There was a single, solitary payphone next to a cardboard sign that read CLAMS IN COOLER. LEAVE MONEY IN JAR.

I parked my car. I went inside the gas station to buy sludgy coffee. I scanned the ceiling for cameras. I talked to the young woman in a red apron at the register; she was deeply incurious about where I'd come from and where I was going at this hour. That was good. I circled the gas station to make sure I was alone. When I was satisfied, I went to the payphone and dialed John.

"Hi, it's Bryn Gillis. I'm a hundred miles south of you. Near Kennebunkport."

"What are you doing there?" John asked me.

"I had to leave New York City," I said, repeating what I'd explained to him in an e-mail. He said he hadn't read my e-mail because he'd been on his boat for a week.

"Listen, Bryn. You can't come here. But I can put you somewhere."

"Is it a CIA safehouse?"

"It's just a house. It's owned by a family friend. It sits empty all winter. Once you're there, we'll get you organized. We'll figure out your next steps," he said.

John gave me instructions. There were so many instructions, and they were so detailed, I had to stop him so I could write everything down. I got my notebook from the car. The obvious stuff about disabling electronics, deleting tracking devices, which I'd already done. But there was more: *Back up your data and put it in storage. Locate agreed-upon checkpoints. Change your license plate number and registration. Get cash. Get your passport.* The list was overwhelming, and it dawned on me that if I'd fled New York City in another direction—if I'd tried to do this on my own, without the help of a friend trained in espionage—I'd be a sitting duck right now.

I hung up the phone and took a heavy breath.

My next stop was a town named Unity, Maine, and without any devices, without GPS, I'd need to find it on a map.

Hours later, I pulled off a wet cement road and parked in a field. The visual markers John had given me—a red barn, two tractors, rolled hay—were ubiquitous. Every town in this part of Midcoast Maine fit that description. I got out of the car and put my keys on the front right tire. Then I got back in the car and waited. I thought, *If I'm in the wrong place, what do I do?* Just then a hard-faced man in a grease-stained jumpsuit emerged from behind a barn. He crossed the field slowly. In one hand, he held a black duffel bag. In the other hand, an object dangled by his side. Hammer or wrench or mallet. As the distance closed between us, I decided he was either going pummel me to death or help me get into hiding.

"Can I take your car? I'll only be five minutes" he said.

He took my car and left me standing in the middle of the field. I saw the car disappear behind a thin curtain of trees. I stood there not knowing what to do with myself. When he came back, the license plate and registration on my car was changed. A Labrador-Husky mix jogged behind him. The dog was lean and athletic, with a shiny coat of black hair, grey face, and grey ears. The dog was jumpy and friendly, he looped through my legs then hopped into the backseat. I told the man to take his dog back. But he didn't.

"The dog goes with you," he said.

I told him that was crazy. I wasn't about to take a dog with me. Not after everything I had to deal with in the coming weeks. I didn't even know where I was going. The man in the jumpsuit really didn't care what I wanted; he had his instructions. As I drove back on the road headed out of Unity, toward coastal Route 1, I eyed the duffel bag in the backseat. The dog was lying with his snout resting on the zipper. *I wonder what your name is...*

Further up Route 1, I passed a campground. There were coin-operated showers. I was in desperate need of a shower. I stopped, parked, and took a change of clothes with me. As I waited for my turn at the shower, with a fleece, jeans, and wool socks in my hand, the dog went berserk in the backseat. I let him out of the car. Maybe he had to pee, I thought. But he didn't. He joined me in line. Then he stood there outside the shower while I was inside. When we got back in the car, I opened saltines and gave him a few crackers. I told him we'd stop for real food later, once we found the address and the boat that was taking us to the island.

An hour later, sun slit through the fog as I drove over a hill into a jewel of a Maine coastal town. The place was remote, quaint, and idyllic. Every house looked empty. The storefronts were dark, closed for the winter. The town hall, the library, the post office—all of it—looked deserted. I drove around for fifteen minutes, and in that time, I didn't see a single car moving or human walking. A battered orange sign pointed me to the town marina. There was plenty of parking there. As I started unloading things from my car, I heard the loud steady thrum of a motor. An old wooden lobster boat, rattling with traps and nets, approached the dock.

"Can I give you a hand loading that stuff onto the boat?" a fifty-something man with red slits for eyes and a meaty neck, in a stained white parka, asked me as he came from behind the plastic sheeting on his boat. "I'm Bob T," he said. As he told me about his boat—it was the oldest Bunker & Ellis in Maine, and though it wasn't pretty to look at, it was reliable, it would get us anywhere in any weather—as he moved boxes and bags from my car into the boat, I could see he was a few drinks deep. He'd had a long winter up here in Maine. His hair was dyed black and falling out in patches. With baby wipes, he wiped engine grease from his hands. He loaded us into the boat. He showed us around.

"Sit here," he said, pointing to a stool near the console.

"Thanks," I said.

"You want a drink?" he asked me, holding out his thermos.

We motored out of the harbor. As we went past a lighthouse, through patches of sunlight and mist, I felt my shoulders relax. The idle of the motor, the rock of boat, was hypnotizing. The horizon widened out. The shoreline behind us receded. I rested my head against the plastic sheeting. I must have dozed off for a few minutes. Because the next thing I knew, we were miles out to sea. There was nothing around us except dark ocean.

"What is that?" I asked, pointing to a twelve-foot-high, red metal can with a wide platform tipping in the waves.

"That's the red nun. Keeps us out of the rocks," Bob said.

The red nun stood up, tipped crooked, then stood up tall again in the waves. As the buoy danced, the bell on top made a hollow sound, a low *gong gong gong*, that drifted across the waves in a haunting rhythm. That there were rocks, danger, where a boat could crash this far out to sea unsettled me. Then I saw the mouth of the harbor. We were approaching land.

Through white mist, an island emerged.

We pulled into a dock at the end of a long pier. Grey shingle, slices of roofline, dotted the distant shoreline. I counted three or four different houses, and I hoped that Bob had instructions on where I should go. He started unloading my cargo. I carried boxes up the ramp, loading them into a rusty wagon. The dog ran ahead and disappeared in the trees.

"Do you know if anyone else lives on the island?" I asked him.

"Not this time of year," he answered.

"Do you know where the house is?" I asked.

"Here's the address John gave me. I believe it's that one right there," he said, pointing with his chin.

I started to climb the narrow dirt road for a better look, I was about to ask Bob for help with something, but when I turned around, he was at the bottom of the ramp. He was on the dock, throwing fenders into his boat and untying ropes from cleats. He started the engine and got prepared to leave.

"Hey, how do I get in touch with you if I need a ride?" I called out.

He cupped his hand behind his ear, to indicate he couldn't hear me.

I went down the ramp. I asked him the same question.

"I don't run my boat time of year," he said.

"Okay, but . . ." I said.

He saw the anxiety on my face.

"If there's an emergency, call me," he said.

"Thank you," I said.

"No problem," Bob said.

That was it. Just like that, he motored out of the harbor, leaving me there on the island alone. As his boat disappeared around a point, I wanted to call out to him. Beg him to stay. *Please, don't leave me here. I have no idea what I'm doing.* I pushed that thought into the recesses of my mind.

I started loading boxes onto the wagon. The dog was way out ahead of me, as I climbed the hill looking for the address Bob had given me. For about a quarter of a mile, there were no houses. Just trees, a steep embankment, and the ocean below. In its silence, its desertion, the island was frightening and sublime. I avoided looking into the choked woods on either side of me. Deep, dark shadows swallowed the space between the trees. Every sound, every crack of every branch, made the hair on my spine stand up.

The air smelled salty and piney.

At the top of the hill, I came to a mailbox. Behind it was a long gravel driveway with thick trees on either side. I pulled the wagon quite a way further before I found the house. It was a three-story, grey-shingle house with dark trim. It had a wide porch in front, and windows that offered a look-through view to the ocean. Behind the house was a gently sloping hill with tall grass. There was a path cutting through the grass. The hill sloped down to the ocean.

I went down the path and stood there, looking at big views of black ocean and grey sky. From this vantage point, I could see weather clouds roll in in from the horizon. I turned to look at the house, where above the third-floor widow's walk there was a whale-shaped weathervane, clanging in the wind. I stood there listening to every sound, trying to get familiar. I walked the property a few times.

The wind picked up. A light rain shattered from the sky.

As I became wet and cold, I was reminded of my death-level exhaustion. I tried to replay the last 72 hours in my head, to piece together the circumstances that forced me out of my comfortable life in New York City to this place—but really, I couldn't. It all felt like a blur. Finally, I turned and walked up the path to the house. I could see the court documents. Fifty pounds of legal briefs for me to review tonight. Or tomorrow. Or the next day. Hopefully, John would arrive before that. *Am I safe here?* I wondered.

A tree split open. The sound exploded in my ears.

Then, a bloodcurdling cry.

Did I hear it? Did I imagine it?

When the dog bounded next to me and started zigzagging, flinging something bloody around in his teeth, I thought my heart would beat out of my chest. Then I saw what it was—it was a bloody seagull with a bloody fish in its beak. The seagull must have hit the tree. The dog was manic, insane, over finding the injured seagull. Blood, feathers, fish scales everywhere. He was about to make dinner for himself when I grabbed him by the collar. My nerves were on fire. My breathing was uneven.

"Come on," I said to the dog. "Let's go inside."

-

The federal investigation began the first week of July 2019.

It was a humid morning, and Helen Hidalgo appeared sick and sweaty. She wore a light red ski jacket over her nursing scrubs. At the magazine kiosk outside the PATH train, I met her. Her wide-set, green eyes were puffy, and she said she'd been suffering allergies. She had a mess of Kleenex in her pocket. She was congested. She stopped to blow her nose.

"Lou Puglisi works in my office," I explained to her. Lou Puglisi was a federal investigator with plenty of experience in these types of cases. "He's about twenty-five, not much older than you. But he's the best there is. He's a super friendly guy. I think you'll feel comfortable talking to him."

"Where are we meeting him?" Helen asked, suddenly nervous.

"A few blocks from here," I said.

We found a quiet coffee shop near the PATH station. When we entered, Lou stood up and greeted us with a warm smile. Helen fell back a few steps. She stood behind me. Lou stood there in his pleated khakis, white button-down shirt, thick glasses, and tried to make casual conversation. Everyone wanted to make Helen feel at ease. But as we got the meeting started, Helen seemed jumpy. Every time the bell jingled over the entrance, she looked over.

"Helen, a federal investigation is a serious thing. It's critical that we get evidence that corroborates your testimony. Golden Care is a highly reputed company, and Angel Woodrow is a beloved CEO. We need evidence that proves to jurors that their impression is wrong. Everything they think about this great man, his great nursing home and hospice company, is *dead wrong*," Lou said.

"Okay," she said weakly.

"If you help us, point us in the right direction, this won't be difficult. Let me give you examples. The transport. You were picked up outside Golden Care in a specific vehicle. We need photos of that vehicle. The plates. The driver, or drivers, if you remember them. You went to restaurants with Angel Woodrow. We can verify these locations. There might be witnesses to prove you were there. The mansion you described in Rockland County with the 'big white gates' that reminded you of a 'Disneyland palace.' I can use phone records to pin your location. We need inventory. The child's playroom—"

Helen stood up. "Can I use the bathroom?"

When Helen was gone, I advised Lou to slow down a bit. Keep the discussion to broader topics, and not delve too much into the logistics of the investigation. "I can tell she's nervous and this conversation isn't helping," I said.

"Sure, no problem," Lou said.

But when Helen returned to the table, Lou dove right in again.

"Helen. You described *specific* objects in the basement. Red circle carpet. Easel with days of the week on quilt squares. Toy bin. Wardrobe with dress-up clothes. Wooden stage. Play chairs. Stuffed turtle. How confident are you about this list?"

"What?" Helen asked.

"Helen. He's just asking if you were to make the list again, would you remember additional items? Or would certain items *not* be on the list?"

"That's not what I'm asking—" Lou intercepted me.

We stepped away from the table to discuss the matter privately. I reminded Lou that it was early in the investigation, and that we needed every bit of Helen's cooperation. We needed her to feel confident about everything she'd told us, comfortable in sharing new details as they emerged in her memory. She was our only conduit to Golden Care, our pillar in the case against Angel Woodrow. If we intimidated her with process, or trial logistics, if we discouraged or overwhelmed her, the case could fall apart. I'd seen it happen before.

"Fine. You lead the discussion," Lou told me.

We returned to the table where Helen was sitting with an empty cappuccino cup in front of her. "Would you like another drink, or a sandwich?" I asked her.

"No thanks," she said.

I began to talk about the schedule, the timeline of the investigation. I mentioned several crucial things we would need.

Lou added, "A federal investigation is a serious thing. I don't mean to say anything to you, Helen, that makes you uneasy, but your list is a little different. What happened to you, well, it's not the standard story we hear—"

I cut in again. "What Lou means is, we will find evidence to back up all your claims. We will put the best people on the job. We will use *any* detail you give us. So, keep the lines of communication open. Keep talking to us. We'll do this together."

Helen gave me an empty look. She blew her nose and stood up.

"Are we done?" she asked.

-

Over the next few weeks, Helen was introduced to the ugliness of a federal investigation. It required her to recount, to dozens of strangers, the worst, most traumatic moments of her life. It was a time-consuming, complex, and emotionally draining process that was filled with uncertainty. I couldn't promise her anything.

Lou and his team doubted that we would find everything we needed. There was a running commentary, a fog of cynicism, each time I passed by their cluster of desks. One morning I heard someone say, "Blue gingham dress with corset. Garter belt. Cowboy says, '*Come and see the barn.*' Western Woman says... I mean, what the hell is this? Did she make this up?"

-

Early August. We needed a second pillar in the case. Helen had stated several times that there were other victims. She cited the blond hair strung in the carpet of the basement, the pile of nail clippings with bits of red nail polish she'd found in the SUV. Helen repeated her accounts of Wanda St. Jean Pierre, the young Haitian woman, and how she'd suffered a nervous breakdown at work, *before* her eventual suicide. We came to believe that Wanda was a victim too, and that if we investigated her relationship with Angel Woodrow, we'd find a cornucopia of evidence. Maybe connections to other victims.

One member of my team took over this part of the investigation.

Sue Katz was a fossil of an attorney. She'd worked at the Southern District longer than anyone. Interestingly, she'd investigated Golden Care for something else a while back; the inquiry had gone nowhere, but she kept her contacts inside the company. Sue had just recovered from thyroid cancer. Her appearance, withered and sickly, gave her the perfect cover to "visit a care facility," to weigh it as a possible retirement location. This allowed her to reconnect with her contacts, which included a nurse, a man named Elvin Winston. He was in fact a retired cop, and he was enormously helpful. He connected Sue Katz with everyone there who knew anything about Wanda St. Jean Pierre, her time at Golden Care, and her relationship with Angel Woodrow. He directed her to a former coworker, Wanda's best friend, Tamara Toussaint. "She's got a lot to say. Go talk to her," Elvin told Sue.

Toussaint, a thirty-two-year-old single mother of two children, was eager to talk to Sue Katz. She invited her to her apartment in East Flatbush. When she opened the door, she said, "I'm surprised the police never asked me anything after Wanda died. I could have told them about all the shit going down at Golden Care."

Toussaint bolted the door behind her.

As Sue started interviewing Toussaint, Toussaint had so much to say that she had to stop a few times to organize her thoughts. "I had all this prepared in my head. But then you showed up, and I started thinking about what they did to her. Just give me a minute," she said.

Toussaint's baby woke up from a nap. She silenced the monitor, then she brought the baby into the room and started breastfeeding him.

She was more relaxed as she continued. "Okay. Here's what I know for sure. Wanda was recruited by one of Angel Woodrow's guys, his name is Carlo R. Anyway, he was a dealer. She was an addict, on and off, but every time she got clean that no good piece of shit came back in her life. He used her drug habit to get her into a bad way. I'm sure I don't need to tell you about it. So, he's the one who introduced her to the boss. Woodrow started taking Wanda on dates. I don't know where they went the first few times, or how many times they went out before it got serious. I know he took her away for the weekend. He took her to his big mansion. He started playing crazy games with her. She'd come back and tell me what they did while she was high. I just thought . . . well, I don't know what I thought. They were doing a lot of drugs. But still. I'd never heard anything like it from anyone."

"What kind of games? Can you be specific?" Sue asked.

"Yeah. Like he made her wear a poodle skirt and little-girl socks," Toussaint said.

"And?" Sue asked.

"And after they dressed up, he'd make her get on a stage. He was the dad. She was his girl. If she didn't act how he wanted her to act—I don't remember exactly what it was—then she'd get in trouble. One of his guys would beat her up. One time they beat the living hell out of her. She came to work with her face all screwed up. Everyone saw it. Everyone noticed it. Another time she didn't play his game, and someone, maybe it was Carlo R., put her in a chokehold. She couldn't breathe. She thought she was going to die right there in the basement of his big house upstate. She said she was going to tell someone, get him in trouble, but she never did," Toussaint said.

"You said basement. Do you know for sure she was taken to a basement?" Sue asked.

"Yes, I'm sure that's what she said," Toussaint said.

The interview went three hours, and Sue recorded every word.

"Thank you. This is hugely helpful," Sue said.

After Sue brought this information to us, our investigation widened to include Wanda St. Jean Pierre, her relationship to Angel Woodrow, and the events surrounding her death. The coroner's report indicated that she had committed suicide by consuming a lethal amount of sodium hypochlorite the morning she was found in the parking lot outside Golden Care. In her bloodstream were other substances, drugs, alcohol, and antidepressants. The police report was thorough; they'd searched her car, taken complete inventory. The clothes on her body, items from her handbag and backpack, the glove box, backseat, and trunk. Everything was listed. Tests had been run, but it wasn't clear for what reason. We went back through everything. We ordered more tests, hoping that we could pin down Wanda's location in the hours leading up to her death.

"Can we get her phone records?" Lou asked one of the Newark detectives who'd been at the scene the day Wanda died.

"I don't see why not," the detective told him.

It took a few days to process everything on Wanda's phone. Sue Katz finally called us into the corner conference room. She spoke with confidence, "Wanda had her phone with her, she called some- one, sent several texts from a location in Rockland County, New York. That cell tower is exactly two point three miles from the house *we suspect* Helen was taken to by Angel Woodrow. Again, we can't be sure of anything until we have exact information. But we're going to get it," Sue said.

-

Once we had enough for a search warrant, we were going to move quickly. We were going to search and seize two of Angel Woodrow's properties, that much was decided. The hours, the min- utes were critical; we knew that Woodrow had eyes and ears in Newark law enforcement and elsewhere. The longer we waited, the greater the chance he could be warned, tipped off by someone. If his properties were cleared out by the time we arrived, if evidence was destroyed or confiscated, there wasn't much we could do to reverse the damage. We could gnash our teeth and make threats. But never again would we have the advantage of catching him unaware, searching and seizing evidence we desperately needed to prove our case.

We picked the Tuesday after Labor Day.

That Labor Day Monday, I stuck around in the city. Lila wanted to join her friends at a water slide park a few hours' drive away, but Nick had just left for a work trip, and I didn't want to do the drive alone. Also, I also didn't want to get caught in hours of Labor Day traffic on the way back from the water slide park. So that morning, I made chocolate chip pancakes for Lila and tried to offer fun activities.

Lila was about to turn nine, and her blond pigtails had turned dark. Her tiny features had grown sturdy in the past year. She had blue-grey eyes like her dad, and the same sweet but stubborn nature. She brooded over her breakfast. The pancakes were burnt at the edges, it was too sunny in the kitchen, the milk tasted wrong, she thought her friends were already at the water slide park having the time of their lives. I offered to take her to the new movie theatre downtown. Then I said we could visit the playground. Or, I said, it would be fun to do a field trip to the Natural History Museum. She sulked to her room to get dressed. She put on green leggings and a puffy paint tank top. She stacked string bracelets all the way up her arm.

"Let's go," she called out halfheartedly.

When we got to the museum, Lila was only interested in the gift shop. I suggested we catch the IMAX show or the planetarium.

"This is stupid. I want to leave," she said.

"Come on, Lila, don't be like this," I pleaded with her.

The summer had taken a toll on her. I'd worked long hours. Two doctors on Nick's team had quit, so he was working long hours. Because he was a cardiologist at Weill Cornell, when he was in surgery he went to the hospital early and arrived home late. We ran out of day camps for Lila to attend in the city. We dropped her at Nick's parents' house in Millbrook, New York, for almost all of August. *Is it okay for a nine-year-old to be away from her parents for a month?* I'd asked Nick. *It's better than hanging around the concrete in August,* he'd responded.

I didn't know if that was true. I hoped it was true. But I felt like a bad mother, and I kept telling myself that once the trial ended, I'd find ways to make it up to her. Maybe I would cut back on my caseload. Maybe I'd apply for a job at a private law firm. Or I could look into a teaching position at a nearby law school. As the familiar debate played in my head, I knew nothing would ever change. My guilt was constant.

Outside the museum, Lila didn't have any idea of what she wanted to do next. Central Park didn't sound fun. The movies didn't sound fun. I finally persuaded her to eat lunch with me at a restaurant a few blocks away, a place that I knew kids loved. Of course, Lila didn't like the restaurant because it didn't have ramen. It had burgers and big ice cream desserts, but she wasn't going to eat short of ramen. I gave her five dollars to exchange for quarters, to play with the stuffed animal machine in the corner. She couldn't get the claw to pick up the striped bear she wanted so she came back for more money until I'd emptied my wallet. When another kid got the bear, Lila stormed back to the table and started crying. She knocked her milkshake over.

"It was an accident," she said, tearing up.

I knelt to clean up the mess. Normally, I would have yelled at her, told her how long my work week had been—how much energy it took to be a working mom, to wake up on your one free day of the week and produce "fun activities" to entertain your family, to cook, to clean, to shop, to schedule, to organize everyone, to listen to non-stop complaints—but I stopped myself. Here I was, laying guilt on her for no reason. She didn't choose to be the daughter of a public prosecutor. I did. It was my choice, and she was living with it.

I pulled her close to me. I held her tight.

We walked across Central Park and found a spot by the water where we could feed the ducks. There was a soft breeze now. The late summer sun burned behind feathery clouds. I fell into a relaxed daze. Lila was happy and entertained. She skipped around the pond. When my phone buzzed in my pocket, I hesitated. But I had to pick it up. It was Lou.

"You ready? I'll pick you up at 4 a.m.," Lou said.

-

Before dawn on Tuesday morning, I watched our crew in black technical tops and puffy windbreakers do a final perimeter check of Angel Woodrow's property. I stood off to one side of the pebble driveway, looking across the acres of wooded property, wishing the sun would rise so that I could get a better sense of the location. This was only one of Angel Woodrow's *many* properties, and it was imposing. Lavish. The structures were massive. Eighteen-foot hedges. Gate house. Carriage house. Pool house. Several structures dotted the wide lawn behind the pool and patio area; there was more here than Helen had described. It was possible she'd never gotten a look at anything outside the house.

We felt good about our preparation and timing.

The stakeout crew had been stationed in the area for a few days. In that time, they hadn't seen anyone enter or leave. Exterior lighting had switched on. Automatic sprinklers. A landscaping crew had done a few hours of work. But that was it. Even the neighbor's property, a few miles down the road, seemed deserted.

I walked in circles, waiting to hear the cue.

My stomach was in knots. I was all but sure we'd get in there to find out that Angel Woodrow had confiscated the place. When the commotion started, boots pounding gravel, shouting, when a glass door broke, I knew they were inside.

I walked over to where a spotlight was pointed through a set of French doors. A crew was going in that side of the house, pulling items out, photographing the items one by one. They pulled a large, coffin-sized wooden crate with a shipping label, a bill of lading, stuck on top. There were customs stamps. It had been ordered from an auction house in Italy. While two guys used a crowbar to get the crate open, an FBI photographer pointed his lens. We all stood there, waiting, as the lid came off the box. Inside, packed in expensive casing and rolls of Styrofoam, was some kind of machine. Polished cherry-wood. A blue cord wrapped tightly on top of the machine. The FBI photographer moved to get a better angle, to snap a few more shots.

"What is that?" I asked the photographer.

He turned to me with something like a smile. "Oh that? That's an electroshock therapy machine. Circa 1940 or '45. Manufactured in Italy. They're not easy to find."

-

That night I walked into my bedroom to find Nick watching baseball. The Mets were playing the Yankees, and he was in a trance, watching the game. He didn't want to talk. That was fine by me. I was dead tired. Also, I was also consumed by the idea that after everything we found inside Angel Woodrow's estate that day, I had my work cut out for me. There was more to the case. Helen's account was the tip of the iceberg.

"You doing okay?" Nick called out to me.

I dropped my clothes into the hamper in our closet. I stepped out to face him, blocked part of the TV, and he gently waved me aside. Nick, at forty-four years old, looked much the same as when we'd first met. He had handsome eyes, dirty blond hair, and he was built like an antelope. No matter how much overate, he never gained weight. In the glow of the TV, I could see his fatigue; he'd been in surgery all day.

"Yeah. Long day. You?" I asked.

"Long day," he muttered. "By the way. Lila's teacher e-mailed us. She's in trouble. She said something to a girl at school. They want us to meet the guidance counselor, but I don't have time this week," he said.

"Are you worried about her?"

"No. Why would I be worried about her? Kids say things to other kids," Nick said.

Typical, I thought. I'm worried. Nick is not worried.

I knew there was more to it. But I couldn't get into a debate right then.

When I brushed past him on my way to the bathroom, he put his arm out. He reached around my waist and pulled me onto the bed.

"I'm filthy—" I said.

"I don't care," he said, putting his nose in my armpit.

-

In U.S. Attorney Sam Applebaum's office, I tried to finalize our draft indictment. Sam was notoriously meticulous and exacting. He didn't approve anything until it was *exactly* to his standard. I knew I was in for a long afternoon when he left and asked his assistant to buy him another bag of sunflower seeds. Several hours later, Sam paced the grey herringbone rug, spitting seeds into a handheld trashcan. He didn't like the asset forfeiture section of the document. He made me read it out loud. Then he stood over my shoulder and nitpicked.

"Read it again. Start there—" he said.

I read it aloud. "ANGEL WOODROW, the defendant, shall forfeit to the United States, pursuant to Title 18, United States Code, Section 1594(c)(1), any property, real and personal, that was used or intended to be used to commit or to facilitate the commission of the offense alleged in Count Two. If any of the above-described forfeitable property, as a result of any act or omission of the defendant (1) cannot be located, (2) had been transferred or sold, (3) has been placed beyond the jurisdiction of the Court, (4) has been substantially diminished in value, (5) has been commingled with other property which cannot be subdivided without difficulty, THEN AND THEREFORE, it is the intent of the United States, pursuant to 21 U.S.C. SS 853(p) and 28 U.S.C. SS 2461(c) to seek forfeiture of any other property of the defendant up to the value of the above property." I paused. "Is that good?"

"No. Erase all that," he said.

A seed dropped onto my keyboard.

-

On October 3, I read the federal indictment aloud to a grand jury—

Over the course of many years, Angel Woodrow sexually exploited and abused women, employees, at his homes in New Jersey, Connecticut, Pennsylvania, and New York, among other locations. That he enticed and recruited, and caused to be enticed and recruited, women and minors to visit his mansions in New Jersey, Connecticut, Pennsylvania, and New York, to engage in sex acts with him, after which he would give them hundreds or thousands of dollars in cash. That in order to maintain and increase his supply of victims, Woodrow paid certain of his victims to recruit additional women and minors to be similarly abused by Woodrow. In this way, he used his public corporation to create a network of victims for him to sexually exploit in locations including New Jersey, Connecticut, Pennsylvania, and New York.

-

The morning of the press conference, I chose a navy-blue pencil skirt and a crisp white shirt. In my bathroom, I changed my blazer three times. I changed from tiny gold hoop earrings to gold studs. I put my hair up. Then I brushed it straight. I slathered on lip gloss. I wiped the lip gloss off my lips.

"Good luck today," Nick called out as I left.

Lila was still asleep; there were teacher conferences that day, which of course Nick and I had to decline for work reasons. Before he went to the hospital, Nick was supposed to drop Lila with a friend's nanny in the park at a certain hour. I worried that he would forget to wake her up in time, forget to feed her, and screw up the schedule. I was about to turn around and remind him of everything that was supposed to happen that morning. Then I looked at my watch. My team was probably waiting. I needed to get downtown.

I rode the E train. I thought about Helen the whole way.

Sam Applebaum and others were outside, at the Greek coffee cart. They were troubleshooting thorny questions that they expected to get from the reporters. It was a blazing September morning, and Applebaum was sweating unnaturally. His collar was soaked. His upper lip was wet. I suggested he move into the shade under a tree, but he said we were going inside. The crowd was arriving. It was time.

"You ready for this, Bryn?" he asked.

We crossed the intersection to our building. I handed him the blue ring binder with all my notes. He scanned it, gave it back to me, and cleared his throat of phlegm. I stepped sideways to avoid the lump of black and yellow goo that flew out of his throat.

The lobby of One St. Andrew's Plaza was packed. People were straining their voices to communicate. There was anticipation, paranoia, excitement in the air. When Applebaum took the podium, the room went suddenly quiet. A shoe screeched on the linoleum. One of the black-blazered security guards nodded his head, winked at me for good luck.

The U.S. Attorney stood tall, hung his left hand on his lapel, and started reading aloud to the cameras: "Today, we will arrest Angel Woodrow, the founder and CEO of Golden Care, Golden Care, Inc., and Dawn Life Hospice Corporation, on U.S. soil—"

The U.S. Attorney looked up, and drilled a look at me.

Chapter Nine. Diary of a Prosecutor on the Run, Part III

Before the sun was up, I started unpacking court documents. It was freezing cold in the house, so I dragged a space heater into the room where I was working. I found wool socks and size ten L.L.Bean boots in the closet. I found an extra puffer jacket to wear. Still, I couldn't get the blood moving through my fingers. I went into the kitchen, switched on the lights, and looked for a coffee maker. There was the prehistoric kind, and I had to remember how to use it. As I poured my first cup of coffee, I burned my lip. I swore loudly and heard the dog move in the next room. He was lying down, sleeping next to the stone hearth. I saw his tail swish as he got up, moved, and lay down in another spot.

I went into the room where I'd set up my things; it was a study off the kitchen with Sister Parish yellow walls, a rope rug, and a pair of green club chairs. The desk was big and functional. Bookshelves lined the walls and gave me a place to look while I was thinking. There was a window that looked out at a garden of frozen ferns. Now I had coffee. I had heat, as the radiator started to pump and hiss. I started moving, working, unpacking boxes, and organizing stacks of depositions, all my notes and notebooks. The juices moved in my brain.

Angel Woodrow had been charged and tried but not convicted. What could I do next?

The Fifth Amendment of the U.S. Constitution states that those acquitted of a particular offense cannot be tried a second time for the same offense. This is the Double Jeopardy Clause. The function of the clause is to prevent a person from being prosecuted twice for the same offense ("No person shall . . . be subject for the same offense to be twice put in jeopardy of life or limb…"). While the concept is simple, the application can be complicated.

Which is to say, there are loopholes.

I needed to explore every one of them.

New evidence leads to new crimes. State and federal courts are different prosecuting entities. Woodrow's lawyers fought to "globally" resolve his liability, but his liability was endless as far as I was concerned. He'd stalked and tortured employees, women like Helen Hidalgo, for years. He'd done it across multiple entities, in multiple jurisdictions. All I needed was a fresh brain to get through this material. If I could find a new angle of attack, a proxy attack, I could get the suspect back into court. I could tie him up for the next year, the year after that, ad infinitum, until he understood that I wouldn't give up. I wasn't going to play his game. He was going to play mine.

Once I understood this, I felt better. I felt alive.

I imagined Angel Woodrow stepping off his private plane in Florida, and one of his lawyers or an aide giving him the terrible news. "Remember that prosecutor, Bryn Gillis? She's coming for you again . . ."

-

October 4 was the first time I laid naked eyes on Angel Woodrow. It was the morning he turned himself in for arrest. His lawyers brought him to the first precinct in Tribeca to face the criminal charges. He emerged from the shiny black doors of the precinct at 8:45 a.m. wearing handcuffs. He was escorted to a black SUV. I'd seen hundreds of surveillance images of him by that point, video clips of him on CNBC, photos taken in trade journals, promotional materials for Golden Care, Golden Care, Inc., and Dawn Life Hospice Corporation. In the Wilkes-Barre nursing home, there was a life-size image of him in the lobby. But nothing I'd seen did him justice. He was *different* when you saw him in person.

Woodrow's frame, five feet and a hundred pounds, was somehow powerful. Quixotic. *Angel Woodrow doesn't look like a sex trafficker,* I recall thinking. When he moved, he reminded me of a stealth deer. He was calm, self-possessed, confident—his public persona was right there for everyone to see—and yet, he had a skulking, lurking quality. His hair was perfect. His skin was flawless and poreless. His eyes looked cut from glass. His grey flannel suit and crisp white shirt, his navy knit tie, his shoes with shoelaces; the outfit was clean, calculated, but not arrogant. As he walked past me his cerulean cufflinks flashed in the sun.

A phalanx of reporters called out questions. With the ease of a man who'd accepted praise his entire life, who had billions in the bank, Woodrow moved to face the cameras. His lawyer, David Worrell, swooped in to stop him from speaking.

As Woodrow neared the waiting car, as he was about to be taken away, a middle-aged woman broke through the crowd. She wore dreadlocks and an orange tropical patterned dress. Leather sandals. Her eyes bulged out of her face as she started yelling at him, "BURN IN HELL YOU FREAK!" Woodrow looked directly at her. He never broke eye contact. He made a motion, soft and quick, touching his hands together. He was praying for her. It stopped her cold. As the car sped away, as the woman in the dreadlocks backed away, the interaction felt like a dream. I'd seen it with my own eyes, and yet I wasn't sure I'd seen it…

"I'm scared to death to face that guy in court" I told Lou.

"Why do you say that?" he asked me.

We were in a noisy diner with red plastic booths now, eating poached eggs.

"Logically, it makes no sense. I've done this before. How many times have I taken violent criminals to court?" I asked.

"I don't know. A lot," Lou answered. He flagged our waitress down. He wanted more butter. His poached eggs were already swimming in grease. He'd emptied the saltshaker on his plate. Now he was going to melt butter on top.

"There's something about him. I can't put my finger on it," I said.

"Well, too late now," Lou said, sliding his phone across the table. Applebaum wanted us back in the office. He wanted to discuss the arraignment.

-

"I'd like to propose bail," Worrell said.

David Worrell, named by the *Journal of Jurisprudence* "The greatest criminal defense lawyer in America," was the same size as his client. With thinning red hair, sunken eyes, a rumpled suit covered in dandruff flakes, he stood across from the judge with his thumb rested under his ear. Always, he spoke in a meditative tone with his head tipped, an indecipherable wobble as he spoke. "Here are the details," he continued.

The courtroom was silent as Worrell read his proposal.

Supervised home detention in Mr. Woodrow's New Jersey residence. Electronic monitoring with a global positioning system. Woodrow would pledge a sizeable bond, $37 million, secured by cash and liquid securities, Golden Care and Golden Care, Inc. stock, preferred equity in Dawn Life Hospice Corporation. In addition, he would pledge a piece of artwork valued at $9 million, two private residences, one in New Jersey and one in Florida. The company's aircraft would be grounded and deregistered until further notice. The arrangements herein would be monitored by a trustee or trustees appointed to live inside Mr. Woodrow's residence, or in one of the guest houses adjacent to the property. Any infractions would be reported to pretrial services and/or the court.

"Does the court accept my proposal?" Worrell laid eyes on the judge.

"I'll permit conditional release—" she said, slamming her gavel.

I turned to Applebaum, Katz and Lou, seated to my left, expecting to see confusion if not open protest on their faces. No one moved, whispered, nor gave me any indication that that they were thinking what I was feeling. Outrage.

We were back in the office. I slammed the door to the conference room.

"Is this a bad joke? He's a danger to those women. Everyone knows that—" I said.

Applebaum sat up and smiled, "Bryn, you've never faced David Worrell. He's just getting started..."

There was a time, truly, when I thought we'd never make it to trial. Worrell threw everything including the kitchen sink at us. One monsoon morning in September, Sue Katz and her paralegal stood over my desk. We still had our raincoats on, we were dripping water all over the place. But another letter had been messengered to us, the third of its kind that week, and we couldn't wait to see what was inside.

"Incredible…" I muttered.

"Unbelievable," Sue said.

"This can't be real," her paralegal said.

It was real. The words were printed in ink.

Worrell wrote to the DOJ, trying to convince them that our investigation, our case against Angel Woodrow, was conducted on improper grounds. He threatened to expose all our "tawdry tactics." He claimed that everything we did in connection with Angel Woodrow, Golden Care, Golden Care, Inc., and the Dawn Life Hospice Corporation constituted "improper federal involvement." He argued the issue "was not appropriately in the heartland of federal law." He cited two cases from the 1980s when Congress required federal law enforcement to meet a threshold of "reasonable suspicion" or "probable case" before launching *any* undercover investigation. He noted dozens of examples of overzealous federal agents not held to this standard who designed plot after plot to frame and incriminate innocent citizens.

He alleged that the prosecutor, "Bryn Gillis" had made false claims to the press, inflammatory comments about evidence. I'd violated the canons of professional ethics. It was his request that the case be barred from federal court jurisdiction. Straight out of William Cheeseman's playbook, the lawyer who defended W.R. Grace in the landmark case *Anderson vs. Cryovac,* David Worrell threatened to sue my boss, the U.S. attorney, Sam Applebaum, if we did not "stand down" in our efforts to "denounce, smear and slander" Angel Woodrow's "good name and reputation." Woodrow's lawyer was willing, happy, to invoke Rule 11. Rule 11, a rarely used provision, stated that a lawyer cannot at his or her whim bring a frivolous and irresponsible lawsuit against an upstanding member of society.

His claims went further.

We'd used "illicit means" to gather material. The source of our investigation was in question. He cited a 2015 infraction where a CIA surveillance program turned up hundreds of images of fishing vessels moving cocaine and heroin into Florida's Gulf coast. The CIA collected and time-stamped these images and handed them as a gift to the FBI. The FBI relabeled the information as its own and passed it to federal prosecutors who went on to make hundreds of drug busts and arrests, leading to thousands of prosecutions in American courts. Finally, a judge questioned the source of the information. Rumors rippled through the press: "The CIA, FBI and federal prosecutors are working in concert to conceal the source of evidence. This is a gross violation of federal law and DOJ guidelines . . ."

The Southern District "was ruthless" and "had no integrity." He said our effort to unseal police records from a 2017 incident whose charges included sexual battery by restraint, forcible oral copulation, resulted in a woman committing suicide in the parking lot outside of Golden Care. In the letter to the Department of Justice, Worrell conceded that Wanda St. Jean Pierre, an employee of Golden Care, was a diagnosed bipolar schizophrenic who went in and out of a state-funded halfway home. There had been abuse in her life, but it did not originate from her employment at Golden Care. There was no indication *ever* that Angel Woodrow or his named co-conspirators were connected to Wanda St. Jean Pierre. There was no evidence that Wanda St. Jean Pierre ever met Angel Woodrow. The letter continued, stating that the U.S. Attorney for the Southern District "has refused to accept this fact" and "they've so doggedly pursued the witness" and "interrogated" the woman in question, that "it is the belief of some family members" that the "U.S. Attorney's office" and our "invasive, probing investigation . . . could have contributed to the death of Wanda St. Jean Pierre."

I stood at my desk after Sue and her paralegal left, reading the letter.

I must have read it three times.

It was typed on cream-colored, double-thick stationery embossed with WORRELL, WITT & NOVAK and addressed to the Honorable Danielle R. Newton, Deputy Assistant Attorney General, United States Department of Justice, 1400 New York Avenue, 6th Floor, Washington, D.C., 20530. If I'd read it, she'd read it by now.

It was undoubtedly making the rounds at the DOJ.

Finally, I worked up the nerve to just call Danielle Newton. Her assistant, Francis Allard, picked up the line. We talked for a few minutes about kids, life as a working mother, traffic in Washington, D.C. Then I jumped into it.

"Are you reading this letter from Woodrow's lawyer? David Worrell?"

"Yeah, it makes no sense," she said flatly.

"So, you agree? It makes no sense?" I asked.

"I have a stack of letters from David Worrell, and none of them make sense. That's his thing," Francis said.

"I've read it three times. Nowhere does the letter explain how we could have caused Wanda St. Jean Pierre's death. The investigation started *after* her death. No one at the U.S. Attorney's Office, no federal investigator, ever questioned her while was alive. How could we have contributed to her death? Does David Worrell not understand the concept of linear time? Is he proposing a time warp?" I asked.

"Bryn. We get it," Francis said.

"Fine, sure, but does Danielle Newton *get it*? Does she agree with me?" I asked.

"She agrees," Francis answered dispassionately.

It was critical, I told her, that I had Danielle Newton at the DOJ on my side. I leveled with her. Working mom to working mom. I said, "Listen. I want to make sure this *bs* letter isn't impacting our case. I want Danielle's assurance."

There was a long pause.

"Yes, I hear you. I need to jump—" Francis said.

A short period of plea bargaining ensued. Worrell persisted with his claims that the investigation was "not appropriately in the heartland of federal law"; he wanted us to lessen the charges or drop them altogether. He offered nothing in return for his demands. Then he offered an olive branch, and it was a strange one indeed.

At a fancy restaurant on Central Park South, over black squid truffle linguini, white asparagus, and a $300 bottle of Puligny Montrachet that no one touched, David Worrell proposed a trade. He named a financier in Greenwich, Connecticut with a $25 billion algorithmic currency and equity derivative hedge fund.

"He's a crook. Everyone knows he fakes returns," Worrell whispered.

"Can you be more specific?'" I asked Worrell.

"What I can tell you is, it's an open secret among Wall Street banks that this guy lies about his returns. He uses every dirty trick in the book to move losses into one sleeve, and gains into another. He trades on whisper information. He front-runs. He bullies employees. He's a fake philosopher. Woodrow knows this financier well. He has information that will help you indict him. But first you need to drop the charges against my client. You set Woodrow free and take this other guy, this financier into your crosshairs…"

Later, Worrell said that he never proposed that trade.

-

As this was happening, a woman, Jane Doe 1, from Dawn Life Hospice Corporation, approached us out of the blue. She'd worked for Angel Woodrow since 2008. She was coerced into acting as an agent, recruiting women from other facilities. In exchange for leniency, she would give us the details of how employees like herself were identified and compromised. She had names, ATM receipts, ledgers. Knowing that someday she could be arrested for the help she gave Angel Woodrow, she'd photographed serial numbers on fifty- and hundred-dollar bills that he'd paid her. Further evidence that she believed she could locate.

She told us that she'd been loyal to Angel Woodrow.

Then, one night after she'd refused him something, when she went to a Rite Aid near her work to buy a few things she needed, headache medicine, tampons, etc., something happened to her inside the store. She was in an aisle shopping when she felt a sharp prick in her neck. It was a pinch, a flash, and when she turned her head, she couldn't figure out what caused it. No one was there. The pharmacist was staring at her. She staggered outside to her car. She passed out on the steering wheel. When she woke up, she was still in her car. It was dark. She felt clumps of loose flesh on her head. She went immediately to the emergency room. The doctor believed she'd suffered a stress attack. She'd blacked out and experienced a bad fall. Probably she'd hit an uneven part of the asphalt, he told her. Jane Doe 1 knew that this event wasn't random. It didn't happen spontaneously. Woodrow was punishing her; he'd sent one of his guys to frighten her. She asked a coworker about the investigation. She got my name from someone, which is how she found my office. If we would protect her, she would testify.

-

At the last minute, I found our expert witness. I walked into a lecture hall at NYU on a Friday morning, and there she was, teaching a room full of students.

She was in her forties, with the body, the confidence of a twentysomething woman. She wore a white silk dress that day, suede heels and gold bracelets. Her thick blond hair was in a ponytail. She stood at a lectern reading her notes.

Dr. Holly Fournier addressed her students, "—sexual games, marital games, power games with bosses, one-upmanship games with friends. These are people experiencing deprivation. Emotional deprivation stems from physical. The infant deprived of handling over a long period succumbs to disease. But what happens to the adult? He experiences *stimulus hunger*. If his reticular activating system isn't sufficiently stimulated, his nerve cells degenerate. Humans play games all day long, even as games ruin their lives, because they're *hungry*. They're hungry to be loved, to be touched . . ."

When I invited her to meet my team at the Southern District, when I brought her into the office the following afternoon, I introduced her as the famous psychiatrist who'd written two best-selling books on Eric Berne's work on transactional analysis.

"How did you get into this line of research?" Applebaum wanted to know.

He was looking at her breasts.

"I've studied every great twentieth-century psychiatrist. Eric Berne's work on transactional analysis is the only work that interests me. Why? I've been asked that many times. I'll tell you why. Because it scares people. *Most* people can't read about transactional analysis. They find it too familiar, and too disturbing," Holly said.

The room was silent as we absorbed that.

Holly offered to "demonstrate" her what she would say to the jury. We rolled a whiteboard into the room. As she got ready to lecture, as she touched her clavicle, her neck, I could see she wasn't afraid to use her body to capture attention. With a blue marker she drew a circle around the word *ALCOHOLIC*.

Husband: We should find out why you've been drinking more lately.

Wife: You're always criticizing me, like my father did.

Husband: Maybe if you talked to someone.

Wife: I'm talking to you now.

Husband: A doctor, I mean.

Wife: I don't like doctors.

"—this game isn't about drinking," Holly lectured. "Whatever the physiological origin, if any, of the need to drink, the game isn't about drinking. It's about three people playing three roles." Holly drew three circles on the whiteboard. In the circles she wrote Victim. Persecutor. Rescuer. "Wife drinks because she needs to be a victim. This is her deepest need. She needs Husband to play persecutor. Doctor, who will come into the game later, will play rescuer. Wife and Husband will learn the doctor has no intention to *rescue* the woman, but that's his role in the game Wife has initiated…"

My phone buzzed in my pocket. Nick, my own husband, was waiting for me in my office with a form he needed me to sign and notarize. Rarely, if ever, did he come downtown to my office during the workday. I told him I'd be finished with my meeting shortly.

Everyone on the team clapped. They were impressed with Dr. Holly Fournier. After she wrapped up her presentation, we thanked her for coming. She followed me onto the elevator and upstairs to my office, where Nick was waiting on the couch. I introduced Dr. Holly Fournier, my new expert witness, to my husband.

As Nick and Dr. Holly Fournier shook hands, their eyes locked.

Somehow, a half an hour went by. I was in and out of my office doing things, making calls, and they were still there chatting. They were laughing about this thing or the other they'd both read in the *New York Times* that weekend. Dr. Fournier stood up and got her bag and coat. Casually, as if it were the most natural, normal thing in the world, she asked, "Do you want to come to my apartment for dinner this Saturday? I'm having friends over. I think you'd both fit in very well."

"We'd love to come for dinner," Nick said, accepting the invitation.

"Great. Seven p.m. Saturday," she said.

-

Saturday, I had other things to worry about.

"Did he *actually* threaten you?" I whispered to Helen Hidalgo on the phone. I was on a bench near the playground in Washington Square Park. It was Lila's best friend's birthday. I'd snuck away for a few minutes to take the call. Nick glared at me, because I was sup-posed to be enjoying the day with Nick and Lila, milling around drinking microbrew beer, fraternizing with parents from her school and singing "Happy Birthday" to the nine-year-old girl who was hov-ered over a triple-decker confetti cake while all the kids yelled and shouted and screamed, "ARE YOU ONE? ARE YOU TWO? ARE YOU THREE? ARE YOU FOUR? ARE YOU FIVE?..." The noise was so intense, I got up and moved away.

"Helen, are you okay?" I repeated.

"No..." she said, crying.

I was worried about Helen. It had been a terrible week for her. Worrell had called her back to repeat a section of her deposition.

"Is this normal?" she'd asked me in the hallway outside the conference room where the deposition was taken.

"No. But he has specific grounds. Just do your best. It will be over in no time," I assured her. Three hours later, we were still in the windowless conference room at Worrell, Witt & Novak, and Worrell had jammed the room with every employee in the building. In front of dozens of strangers, two videographers, Helen was made to repeat the details of a night she'd barely survived.

"The night of March 10. Can you tell us what happened?" Worrell asked.

"I wasn't feeling good," Helen started.

"Please stick to the facts," Worrell said.

Helen had clocked out a little after 9 p.m. She was feeling nau-seous, so she told Woodrow's driver she didn't want to take a ride with him. They offered to take her home. Instead, they took her to a barbeque restaurant for dinner. They made her drink something that she thought was drugged.

"Please stick to the facts," Worrell interrupted her.

She continued. She said she'd felt woozy as she climbed back into the car. They traveled upstate to his mansion with the white gates. "That night he asked me to wear roller things in my hair. Plaid slippers. He wore a bathrobe and had something tied around his neck. He said I was his wife. That I was an alcoholic. He stood across from me and got angry. *We should find out why you've been drinking more lately...* and I was supposed to say, *You always criticize me like my father did...*" The red pin light on the video reflected in Helen's eyes. Her hands were still.

Following the deposition, Helen moved in with her sister and her sister's boyfriend, because she felt unsafe living by herself. The new apartment was in a sketchy area. She was calling me now, on a Saturday, to tell me she'd been threatened. Nearly attacked.

"Helen, tell me *who threatened you*," I said.

"I went out last night with them [her sister and sister's boy-friend]. It's the first time I've been out since all of this started. I saw a man going through my trash, but I thought he was a homeless guy. Then I saw a car parked across the road. We went to this taco place in Jersey City. We ate and danced and had a few drinks. My sister's boyfriend had to go to work then, so he offered to drive us home. When we got to his car, two guys came out and beat him up. I saw the guy. He was the same guy who'd been going through my trash," Helen sobbed.

"Did you call the police?" I asked.

"No, I called you..." she said.

"Did you get it on video?"

"No..."

"Helen. Listen to me. It's a federal crime to intimidate wit-nesses. I highly doubt that they would risk doing something like this. But if it makes you feel better, I'll send someone over now. If it happens again, I'll take it up in pre-trial. You're one hundred percent safe. Do you understand?"

"Okay," she said, sobbing.

When I hung up the phone and returned to the birthday party, Nick was upset. He was really pissed off at me. I could see it on his face. I resented that he resented me for doing my job. This case, *United States v Angel Woodrow*, was not a small thing. It made every major news outlet. Pundits everywhere were talking about it. It was only a few weeks until trial. Of course I couldn't ignore my phone. I said something to this effect, and he turned away. He wouldn't give me eye contact.

"You know what? Why don't you go to that woman Holly Fournier's dinner party without me tonight," I said sarcastically, harshly.

"Fine. I will," he said, walking away.

I went home and made a few calls. It didn't occur to me that Nick would take me up on the offer. It never occurred to me he would *actually* go to the dinner party alone, that he would sit next to Holly, that he would drink a lot, that she would touch his arm or his leg and invite him to stay over.

-

The first week of October, I began drafting my opening arguments. From sunup to sundown, my team interrupted me to discuss the newest problem. Amidst a backdrop of endless, constant, relentless interruptions, I tried to focus. They burst into to my office, sweating and complaining, losing their composure, cursing, moaning, abhorring whatever pre-trial fiasco Worrell was stirring up. Verbal threats, requests, and injunctions. Warnings. Amendments.

Delays. More threats. Threats of delays. Angry missives from the judge. He-said-she-said-I-said-she-said-the-judge-said accusations that would land us all in disbarment. Everyone was in a full panic. It was as if they could feel a hurricane coming, didn't want to be in its path, didn't want to be anywhere near the storm when it landed. Try as I did to shut my door and concentrate, I couldn't.

I took my laptop to another floor.

I found a cement hole in a storage hallway, with one window. The smell of burning grease from a chicken restaurant below seeped into my hair and my clothes. Even my legal pads stunk. I was fine to endure the smell, the hardship, if it meant I could focus. But then Sue Katz figured out where I was working. She pulled a folding chair into that smelly room, complained about what David Worrell had said to her and then to the judge that morning, and gnawed her index finger until it bled.

I called Nick to tell him that I needed to check into a hotel and work that weekend.

I wouldn't be home.

"We had plans Saturday and Sunday. We promised Lila that we would take her to that water slide park, and we promised my parents we would visit. You haven't been *here* in weeks. Are you really going to a hotel to work?"

I didn't know what to say. I didn't know how to apologize.

Nick asked quietly, "Bryn, how long is this going to last?"

Then he hung up on me.

I checked into the Conrad Hotel downtown. In a 400-square-foot white box with a futon-looking bed and a stained herringbone carpet and black-and-white poster art, I set my laptop on the desk. I guzzled an energy drink. I tried to write my opening arguments. I wrote a few words. Deleted everything. I went downstairs for a double espresso. I wrote. Deleted. Wrote. Deleted. I went on like this until I had an opening argument I could live with. I stared at the work I'd completed—*Here it is! I've written the entire thing*—then I decided the language could be more concise. I changed a few things. Then I wiped the screen clean.

At one point, I entered a deep depression.

The days, the months, the case, the injured women—it swirled in my head.

I felt sick.

I needed to go back through everything. My notes the first day I met Helen. I needed to revisit each turning point in the investigation. Fill in holes. Reorder the arguments. If I didn't do it this way, I'd never get to the center. I moved to the bed, fell asleep, and woke up in sweat-soaked pajamas. In dawn twilight, with caffeine still pumping through my system, my fingers moved fast. I wrote, "Your Honor, members of the jury, my name is Bryn W. Gillis, representing the prosecution . . ."

-

In the last hour of sleep, the morning before trial, I had a terrible nightmare. I was in the defendant box. Dr. Holly Fournier was examining me. She was asking me difficult questions, questions that I couldn't answer. Every time she didn't like my answer, she stuck something sharp into her neck. A pen. A letter opener. There was blood spurting. She demanded that I explain the game *Now I Got You, You Son of a Bitch*, and I kept mumbling. "Victim, Aggressor. Jealous rage. Adult-Adult. Adult says, *See, you have done wrong.* Other Adult says, *Now that you draw it to my attention, I guess I have.* Internal Psychological is Rage. External Psychological is Avoids

Own Deficiencies. Biological. Belligerent Exchange. Ipsisexual. Existential. Message: People Can't Be Trusted. AM I RIGHT?"

I woke up shouting, sweating. My alarm was blaring.

-

"Where is everyone?" I asked a guard outside the courthouse.

The street, the stairs of the courthouse, were completely empty. There was only a homeless man blowing his nose into the fountain.

"You're early," he said.

But I figured the rest of my team would also be early.

I climbed the steps, dumped my keys and wallet and phone into a plastic tub. I took off my coat and went through the metal detector.

"Nope," he said.

"I haven't seen anyone," another guard told me.

I went upstairs and sat on a window bench. I started to review my notes, mouth my lines, when my phone buzzed. A notification. Then two notifications. Three. Four notifications. Then someone was calling me. It was Lou. Sue called. Then Sam Applebaum called. I didn't pick up the phone right away because I understood that a piece of news, a headline had hit. I wanted to read and absorb whatever it was. As I read the article, my heart stopped.

...a prosecutor from the Southern District is arresting and incarcerating victims who get scared and refuse to testify in court. Court Watch NYC, volunteers who monitor New York's criminal courts, issued a report showing that in the months before trial, this prosecutor arrested and jailed victims after they refused to testify for the prosecution. The victim took a video of her boyfriend being pulled out of a bar in Jersey City and beaten in an alley by undercover cops,

until she agreed to testify. Another victim was drugged in a Rite Aid near her work, dragged into her car, and threatened. She was released after she agreed to testify. She is scheduled to appear in court this week.

-

The last game Angel Woodrow played was with me.

-

Some seventeen pages of my notebook is devoted to the angst, the confusion I felt in those hours. Things fall apart, the saying goes. Literally, everyone fell apart around me. Every pillar of the case crumbled. Applebaum felt pressure to step back, walk away, denounce our efforts altogether. Danielle Newton from the DOJ called to tell us she had "grave concerns" about our strategy, our tactics. She wanted to see us right away. Nick stopped coming home. He said if I was going to stay at a hotel, he was going to stay at a hotel. At least until I figured out my priorities. Did I want to be a committed mom? A committed wife? This, he said, a few hours after he'd had a great orgasm in Holly Fournier's bed.

"She's my expert witness," I said, after he told me.

"So what does that have to do with anything?" he asked.

"I don't know," I said.

Because I didn't know. Our marriage had been fine until it wasn't. Or maybe I was blind, and it wasn't fine. Either way, I couldn't talk. Sue Katz had just gone back into the hospital, she was sick. Lou was pulled onto another case. Two Assistant U.S. Attorneys who had literally no preparation were assigned to help me while things were figured out. Jane Doe 1 called me, e-mailed, then walked into my office to tell me she was "afraid" to sit in the witness box after everything that had happened. She would not, under any circumstance, face Angel Woodrow in the courtroom. Another cooperating witness said the same thing that afternoon. As night fell over the Hudson River, as I walked alone, as a shadow started behind me and followed me up the path, over the walking bridge, around the block and back onto the same walking path—it occurred to me—I wasn't safe either.

-

Around that time I realized that I needed to leave New York. That's how I got to this island.
I'm writing it now at 4 a.m. just to make sense of it again.

-

"John? Are you coming to the island?" I type in a chat box.
I wait. No response. He could be anywhere in the world. I'm hoping, maybe stupidly, that he left Deer Isle and will be arriving any minute. I've done my morning routine. Push-ups, v-ups, stretches, pull-ups in the doorframe. There was an inch of frost on the window when I committed mentally to go down to the beach for my cold plunge. I walked outside with a down jacket zipped over my towel. I walked the path toward the narrow stairs. Hanging over me is a bruised, black sky. In the distance, the waves toss restlessly.
Get in the water, do it quickly. Get it over with, I repeat to myself.
It was the third day in a row I'd managed to get my entire body into the water. It was helping my back. It was helping my mind. It was helping everything.
I wrapped the towel tighter, descended the beach. The salt wind stung my face. The rocks were ice-slimed, covered in barnacles

and frozen brown-green seaweed. Everything was thawing, crack-
ing, popping under my feet as I made my way. Twenty feet out in the
water, a loon floated by and disappeared behind a white spire of mist.
I took a deep breath. I put a toe in the water. I dropped my clothes.
I heaved ten breaths—*in, out, in, out, in, out, in, out, in, out*—then I
started walking forward. *You're dying,* I thought, as the water crawled
up my shins, my knees, my hips. Do ten seconds. I counted to myself.
Nine, eight, seven—

A man came up behind me and grabbed my shoulder.

I screamed bloody murder.

-

The man in the neoprene suit behind me is not a dream.

He's not a hallucination.

He's shouting at me as I sprint over the rocks, falling, slipping,
something sharp goes into my hand, my forearm, my face, as I fall
forward. Blood.

All I can think is: I've strung a duffel to the pine tree left of the
mailbox with a weapon, passports, and cash. It's a quarter mile to the
mailbox, fifteen feet to the duffel, and fifty feet to a trailhead across
the road. That trail runs a mile through the woods to the north side
of the island. There it nosedives off a cliff into the ocean. Left is a
white clapboard church. The church has cell service. If the weather is
clear, then I can arrange a pick-up from below that ledge. If the fog is
thick or thunder clouds roll in, if the boat can't reach shore—if I get
lost, poisoned, drowned, or shot in the back by a sniper—I copied
every document to an encrypted flash drive and taped it to the electrical panel inside room 12 at the Acadia Mountain Inn. This I'll tell
my friend with the blue boat when he arrives.

"Bryn…"

I'm crawling to my feet, trying to get up, to run.

"Bryn…for god's sake…"

I realize, I know that voice. I know him. I'm not in danger.

I turn and hit him hard in the chest.

"I'm sorry, I'm so sorry—" John says. "I went into the house. You weren't there. I called your name twice as I came down the steps. I didn't realize you didn't hear me."

-

Now I'm in the kitchen with the hunting knife strapped to my belt. It's the only thing that makes me feel better. I'm shaking so hard, still, that John pours me a stiff drink.

"You okay now?" John asks.

"No," I say firmly, swallowing the vodka. It burns my throat.

John Haas, my CIA friend, at long last, here on the island. He's still wearing his black foul-weather gear, and part of his neoprene suit. He's dripping water all over the floor. His blood-flecked eyes, his winter-white hair, his strong jaw, his concerned, amiable smile—he looks at me kindly, waits for me to feel better.

"I'm going to sit down," I say finally.

"Why don't you have another drink? I'll bring in wood and light a fire. I brought groceries, dinner, all of it. It's in my boat. Let me shower and change into dry clothes, then I'll get started. You need to relax. Can you do that?" John asks.

"Thank you for coming," I manage to say. "Even if you gave me a heart attack."

John smiles, doesn't laugh, and I can tell he's concerned.

He wanders around. Then he stands in the door of the study where my depositions lay all over the carpet, where the desk is a mess of work and empty coffee cups. He looks at me.

"Bryn, are you going to be okay if I leave you here? If I run back to the boat for ten minutes?"

"I'm fine," I say. "I've been alone all week. What's another ten minutes?"

The dog jogs out of the house behind John.

A fire is crackling in the living room now, and I've had a full glass of vodka. I sink into the deep pillows on the couch. Through the bay window, I can see John move down the path to make his way back to the beach. His little boat, his tender, is anchored below. It's strange that I hadn't seen his boat when I went down to the beach. Maybe he'd anchored it on the shoreline near the point. Maybe I'd been looking in the other direction. And where is his big boat? It must be on the dock where Bob Trawley had dropped me. But why had he left it there? These insipid details, questions, are swimming around in my head as I finish my drink. I think about pouring more vodka. The panic, the fear, is dissolving. The alarm is seeping out of my muscles. My head feels heavy. I lie sideways and put my feet up. The best thing, I think, is to wait until John comes back in ten minutes. Then I'll ask him all my questions.

-

It was dark when I lifted my head from the couch. The fire was out. There was one light on in the kitchen, and the refrigerator door was ajar. I walked around in a daze, poured myself a glass of water. I wondered why when John came back inside, he hadn't thought to wake me. We'd planned to have dinner together. Where was the food he'd brought? Had he just gone upstairs to bed and not told me? I climbed upstairs and checked the bedrooms. The bed was made in every bedroom except the one I was sleeping in. *Odd*, I thought. Maybe he sleeps on his boat? I went downstairs, used a burner phone to call him. He didn't pick up.

I looked outside at the dark outline of trees, the long gravel driveway that turned into the dirt road leading down to the dock. I had a terrible feeling.

I sensed something was wrong.

My fleece was in a dry seal backpack, so I grabbed it, put the hunting knife inside, and jogged down the long driveway to the road. I resolved not to look at the choked woods on either side of me, or the tree shadows jumping around. Huge pockets of darkness lay ahead. The few houses along the road stood like black sentries. I jogged down the hill, toward a single feeble light hanging over the end of the dock.

I started running when I saw his blue boat thrashing around in the waves. The lines were slack, it was loose from the dock, and the storm lights were flashing.

"John?" I yelled a few times. No answer.

Holy shit, I thought, *Maybe he fell. Maybe he had an accident?*

I couldn't think how old John was. Seventy? Seventy-five? But he was in incredible shape. Was it possible he had a heart attack? Maybe he slipped? I was at the edge of the dock, wondering whether to run back to the house to call 9-1-1 or the Coast Guard. Then I decided it was faster to call from the radio on his boat. Or send up an SOS signal, a flare, to any fishing vessels in the area. The boat was only a few feet off the dock from where I stood, but it was a big boat, unwieldy, and though I had the line in my hands, I couldn't pull the boat alongside the dock. The water was too choppy. The stern was crashing diagonally, moving backwards toward sharp rocks sticking from the water. I could jump to it. It was about four feet away. I was pulling the bow line with all my strength, getting ready to jump, when it happened.

Two hundred pounds of flesh hit me from behind.

I plunged headfirst into the water.

Immediately, there was pressure on top of me. An arm came around my throat. My head hit something hard; it was the side of the boat. We were underwater, between the boat and the dock. When I came to my senses, realized what was happening, I dove vertically, trying to get deeper in the water. I touched bottom. Someone had my arm. I twisted and kicked away, under the hull of the boat. The water was dark and murky enough. When I was only a few feet away, I was in the clear. But I didn't know how long I could hold my breath down there. Maybe two minutes? I saw the gleam of the motor. I came up thrashing for air. I filled my lungs, pulled myself on the back platform the boat so I could get a clear look inside. I saw him. There was John. He was lying flat. There was no blood. But he wasn't moving. He was seriously injured, or unconscious. I was about to yell to him, about to pull myself onto the back of his boat, when someone grabbed me and pulled me back under the surface.

I thought I would drown.

I blacked out, felt myself sinking, falling, losing consciousness. Then I was swimming. I let the current take me. I went as far and as fast as I could, and when I came up for air, when my head emerged, I was way, way out from the shoreline.

I could see the feeble light over the dock, small and disappearing.

I couldn't swim back. Fear consumed me.

My legs, and then my chest, hit a hard metal object. I didn't know what it was, but I held on for dear life. It was the red nun. The signal buoy. The base was slimy and slippery and not easy to grasp. It was tipping back and forth in the waves. The current had taken me out. I was all the way out in the ocean, beyond the mouth of the harbor.

Not easily, I pulled myself onto the ledge.

The hollow *gong gong gong* of the bell filled my ears.

Blackness, slowness, confusion gripped my body. Panic and fear of hypothermia flashed in my brain. I looked at my fingers. They were frozen blocks of flesh. I was about to lay my head down to rest, to swallow air, when I realized, I was wearing my backpack. I still had my dry seal backpack on my back.

I couldn't get the zipper open with my frozen fingers. When I finally did, I rooted around until I found a lighter. A folder stuffed with paper. Memos. "Part and object of the conspiracy that Angel Woodrow, the defendant…" that page was filled with typos. I ripped a corner off the memo. I lit it with the lighter, and it made a tiny flame. I stuck the flame under my fleece, near my stomach, and it gave off heat for a few seconds. I tore off another scrap. I lit it, held it near my stomach. I pulled the fleece over my knees and made a tent. As the waves rose, I looped my belt through the metal bar on the buoy, to secure myself. *If the weather holds, I can survive another hour…*

Acknowledgments:

To the English department at Milton Academy and David "Red" Smith in particular. You taught me the road to hell is paved with dangling modifiers and split infinitives. To the writers who pulled me along: Heather McGhee, Ben Forkner, Joel Schumacher, Hugo Lindgren, Alexandra Wolfe, Maggie Cohn. For the mindset: Phil Stutz, Christine Goulding.

To the people I love the most, thank you for the time to write: J, C, E, S, G.

Made in the USA
Columbia, SC
12 May 2024

ea25e099-3829-4894-88d4-a6da100a7036R01